THE MANTON
REMPVILLE MURDERS

First Published in Great Britain 2014 by Mirador Publishing

Copyright © 2014 by Julian Worker

First edition: 2014

A copy of this work is available through the British Library.

ISBN: 978-1-910530-06-1

Mirador Publishing
Mirador
Wearne Lane
Langport
Somerset
TA10 9HB

The Manton Rempville Murders

An Inspector Knowles Mystery

By

Julian Worker

Mirador Publishing
www.miradorpublishing.com

Other Books By Julian Worker

Julian's Journeys
40 Humourous British Traditions
Sports The Olympics Forgot
Travel Tales From Exotic Places Like Salford

An Inspector Knowles Mystery
The Goat Parva Murders

Chapter 1

Detective Sergeant Rod Barnes surveyed the remains of Manton Rempville monastery with incredulity. He'd heard that a hundred thousand pounds had been spent on preserving the ruins and he couldn't understand why anyone would do such a thing. Ruins were ruins for a reason. The natural order of things, in Barnes' mind at least, was gradual decay – preservation only delayed the inevitable, like applying skin cream to wrinkles or a new coat of paint to a rusting car. Besides, the ruins were open to anyone and there was no entry charge, so they were never going to get their money back.

Barnes stiffened slightly as he saw Detective Inspector Colin Knowles' Land Rover chug into the car park and lurch to a halt too close to Barnes' Morgan sports car for his comfort. He glanced down at the body and thought that Knowles, his boss, would find this crime scene interesting indeed. Barnes had heard Knowles was on a new diet and that his latest culinary delight was vegetable kebabs cooked on his nearly new barbecue even in the depths of autumn.

Taking care not to get his highly polished shoes muddy, Barnes walked across the uneven grass as a low, cold wind whipped across the historical site, slightly disturbing his short, brown hair. He hadn't seen much of Knowles in the past month as they'd both been away on holiday at separate times since the murders in Goat Parva. As he came towards him, Barnes noticed that even though the Inspector had lost weight, he still wasn't able to tuck his Marks and Spencer shirt into his trousers.

"Good morning, sir, how are you today?"

"Fair to middling, Barnesy old son, the diet's working well, nearly fifteen pounds lost." Knowles gripped his much reduced stomach with some pride.

"How's the gym going?"

"Gradually doing more on the treadmill, lifting a few weights, and getting some stretching done on those large blue balls they have. That's not easy – those balls are bouncy as hell – I almost fell off the first few times I tried to lie on the thing. Anyway, not only can I see my toes now, but I can almost touch them too."

"That's good to hear, sir. The trick to keeping the weight off is by committing to a lifestyle change rather than thinking you're on a diet."

"Good point, Sergeant, lifestyle sounds very magazine-like though, very posh Sunday newspaper, but I know what you mean. Anyway, who do we have over there?" Knowles pointed in the direction of the photographer and Forensics team, who were investigating the crime scene.

The two men started to walk over to the eastern wall of the monastery's refectory where the body had been found an hour earlier by Bingo the retriever, out on a long walk with his owner Adelaide Hills from Goat Parva. Both dog and owner were well known to the police from a few weeks before when Bingo had made a habit of finding bodies in the early morning.

"According to his credit cards, his name is Edward Pritchard; we are just running some computer checks to find out where he lives. It's how he's been killed that you will find interesting, sir."

With his hands in his trench coat pockets huddling against the cold, Knowles stood on the wall and looked down at the body lying on what would have been the refectory floor. Edward Pritchard had been run through with a sword and the handle was sticking out of his back on the left-hand side. Knowles smiled at Dr. Crabtree, the forensic doctor, who was examining the body.

"Dr. Crabtree, we have a real sword being used as a murder weapon?" Knowles would have rubbed his hands with glee if they hadn't been warming up in his pockets.

"We do indeed, Colin, a very real sword. This is a heavy cavalry sword with a straight blade with one cutting edge whereas the other side has been thickened for greater

2

strength. The blade is around three feet in length. It directly penetrated his heart and he would have died instantly."

"Any prints on the handle?" Knowles looked hopeful when he said this.

"We'll check back at the lab, Colin, can we move him now?"

"Yes, that will be all I think. We'll be back at the station in an hour or so; could you have something by then in terms of fingerprints, time of death, and any ideas on a profile of who could have done it?"

"We'll try, Colin – no promises, but we'll try."

"I presume the person who murdered Edward wasn't aware of the type of sword they were using," said Barnes, "because that's a sword for slashing people with, not for running them through."

"So, you would have expected a murderer who knew what he was using to have hit Edward here in the neck with the sharp side," replied Knowles.

"Yes, sir, that's correct."

"So we're looking for an ignorant murderer then? We show the suspects the sword and ask them how they would kill someone using the sword and those who opt for the neck slash are innocent?"

"They might be bluffing, sir, so we shouldn't just use that as a method of elimination from our enquiries," said Barnes, playing along with Knowles' quite acerbic sense of humour.

"OK, we'll just confine ourselves to telling the murderer, when we catch him, that he/she murdered Edward here in the wrong way. So where could the sword have come from? It's not the sort of weapon you can easily conceal."

"The nearest house is Manton Rempville Hall – you can see it just poking through the trees over there. That might be the best place to start."

"Agreed – they probably maintain an assortment of weapons to keep the staff subdued and repel invasions by the local peasants in times of crisis. We should go there after visiting our oldest friend in Goat Parva, Mrs. Adelaide Hills, and her bundle of fun, Bingo."

"It's just like old times, sir."

"Indeed it is, Barnesy. I just hope that this is the only body Bingo finds in this murder investigation."

========

Barnes and Knowles drove their vehicles back to Goat Parva and parked outside The Cottage, the imaginatively named residence of Adelaide Hills and her retriever, Bingo.

"Well, here we go again, sir," said Barnes as he knocked on the door and heard the mad barking of Bingo inside.

"Bingo is in fine voice today, oh how I have missed those desperate notes of happiness from our favourite retriever," replied Knowles, "give me a cat any second of the day."

"And how is your kitty, Gemma?"

"I've bought her a male friend from the animal shelter in Madeley. His name is Freddie and he knows who's boss in our house. He tried to pick a fight with Gemma on his second day in residence and he won't be doing that again. She has a mean straight right and she scratched his nose quite badly. He was so upset; he hides behind me whenever he can…oh, here is Mrs. Hills."

Adelaide Hills opened the door and flashed a relieved smile as she recognised the two officers. She looked slightly greyer than the officers remembered her from earlier in the year. Her husband had died a few years previously in a camel dismounting accident and she now lived alone, apart from Bingo. She was always wary about opening her door.

"Sergeant Barnes and Inspector Knowles, what a surprise! I rather thought we'd never meet like this again, but how wrong I was."

"Well, we thought the same thing, but Bingo seems to have a nose for dead bodies," grinned Barnes.

"You won't be having me followed on my morning walks will you, Inspector Knowles?"

"Not yet, Adelaide, not yet. Could we come in? It's a bit cold out here."

"Of course, where are my manners – Bingo, stop there and allow these two gentlemen to pass by."

Bingo withdrew slightly, but eyed the shoes of the two policemen with great suspicion. As usual, the six foot three inch Barnes had to duck his head to get through the low doorway, but Knowles was a good six inches shorter and didn't have the same problem.

Knowles and Barnes sat on Adelaide Hills' settee in her living room and declined her offer of a cup of tea. Barnes straightened his trousers and rubbed a speck of dirt from his left shoe. Knowles just looked crumpled.

Barnes began, "Adelaide, you and Bingo were walking this morning near Manton Rempville when something quite familiar happened."

"Yes, Sergeant, Bingo started barking when we were walking through the monastery grounds and straining at his leash; I followed him into the refectory where we saw that man who had been stabbed with the sword."

"Did Bingo take anything?"

"No, he was on a tight leash, and I have learned my lesson. I phoned you from the scene of the crime and waited until your local constable arrived from Norton-juxta-Wychwood and then went home. Bingo didn't pick up anything from the scene and didn't take any clothing." Adelaide Hills smiled as she knew the officers couldn't rebuke her this time.

"Things are improving – now, did you see anyone in the area of the monastery, Adelaide?"

"I did, Sergeant. There were three young men horsing around as they walked through the trees away from me towards Manton Rempville Hall and also a youngish couple sitting on a fence by the monastery car park having an animated discussion. There were no vehicles in the car park, so I presume they'd walked there too. I also heard an older couple arguing about some money-related subject such as wills when I was walking back here after the constable had arrived."

"And how old were the young men and the youngish couple, would you say?"

"The young men were around twenty and the youngish couple were slightly older, say around twenty-five, but no older than that."

"When you say the young men were horsing around – what were they doing?"

"They were fooling around, pretending they had swords and fighting each other." Adelaide Hills waved her arm in front of her, parodying a fencer.

"That's a very strange coincidence, isn't it?" interjected Knowles, leaning forwards.

"I suppose so, Inspector, but could their horse-play and the murderer's modus operandi be connected, do you think?"

"We'll be heading to the big Hall later on today, so we'll find out who you saw and why they were acting in that manner."

"Well, I hope I have been of help, Inspector, and do call again if you need to ask any more questions."

"We will certainly do that, Adelaide, thank you." Barnes and Knowles stood up and Knowles tried to pull the dog hairs from his trousers without much success. He glared at Bingo.

As the two policemen left, Bingo looked rather sad. Neither of the two men had patted him on the head as they passed.

========

Knowles and Barnes drove back to Scoresby station and immediately headed to the Forensics laboratory, hoping that Dr. Crabtree would have some news for them.

"Well, Colin, I don't have that much to tell you, really. You know some of it already. Stabbed in the back with some force by someone slightly taller than the five foot seven inch victim – the blade has followed a slightly downward trajectory – victim died instantly and fell in a heap on the ground causing the blade to buckle and bend slightly, so that the murderer was unable to remove the sword cleanly although they had a good go, causing the exit wound to be very messy indeed. There are no fingerprints on the sword whatsoever."

"Really? So the murderer was wearing gloves," said Knowles, "go on, Dr. Crabtree."

"We found a red thread on the hilt of the sword, which looks as though it has come from a sheet or towel used to hide the sword from view."

"No great surprise there," said Barnes, "few people could carry a sword without alerting suspicion of some kind."

"Whereas carrying a large red towel is perfectly normal and wouldn't be in any way uncommon," replied Knowles, "although it was probably carried in a bag for the most effective disguise. What material is the thread?"

"I think it's cotton, Colin, we can have it analysed for you."

"Yes please, Doctor, I like to be thorough when analysing evidence."

"Of course, Colin, that won't be a problem."

"And now the all important question – what was the time of death approximately?"

"Well, I am almost certain the time was 11:06 p.m."

"Give or take an hour or so?" said Barnes.

"Give or take thirty seconds," said Knowles. "The doctor is indicating that the victim must have smashed his watch when he fell dead to the ground – are there any fingerprints on the watch?"

"We'll have to check, Colin, and let you know when it's been dusted."

"Thank you – I wonder whether he would have smashed his watch, though, if he fell onto the grass."

"The watch face was broken by something" said Dr. Crabtree, showing Knowles the watch enclosed in a plastic evidence bag.

"Indeed it was, but there's no indication it hit the grass, no soil, no colouring of green. Were there any stones lying around where he landed?"

"Let's look at the photos, shall we?"

The men walked over to the doctor's table and examined the photos that showed the ground around Pritchard's left hand.

"There are no stones around where his left hand and wrist would have landed, so what could he have hit the watch on?" pondered Barnes, stroking his short beard.

"There's nothing obvious, is there, so either the killer did it to fool us or it was broken before he was killed," replied Knowles. "Doctor, what do the other signs tell us about his time of death?"

"They more or less fit with the watch. I would have put the time at between 10:30 and 11:30p.m. last night. Perhaps 11:45p.m. at the outside."

"Interesting, so I wonder why half-an-hour could make so much difference, if the murderer knew the body wouldn't be found until the morning?"

"It has to be to establish an alibi, sir – I can prove I was with Person X at 11:06p.m. and they will verify that, whereas half-an-hour earlier or later and that alibi would not hold."

"Indeed, Sergeant, we shall have to ask our questions very carefully when we meet our suspects."

"You have some suspects already, Colin? That was quick work." Dr. Crabtree readjusted his glasses with some surprise.

"Well, I suppose I shouldn't call them suspects yet, as I haven't even met them, but I was referring to the people who live at the Hall near Manton Rempville. Adelaide Hills saw some people behaving suspiciously when she discovered the body and they must have all come from the Hall."

"Try not to bring class politics into the conversation, Colin, especially when there's a case to be solved."

"Right, wait until afterwards, you mean?"

"Something like that, yes, and don't forget that Sir Michael Johnson, who owns Manton Rempville Hall, is a personal friend of the Chief Constable, and any complaints will go straight to that level."

"Thank you for the warning, Dr. Crabtree, I will bear what you say in mind, but I do have to find a murderer after all and that's the main aim of my investigation. Now, do you have a nice picture of the sword that I can show to the people at the Hall, preferably one that doesn't show it sticking into Mr. Edward Pritchard? That would be quite tasteless, wouldn't it, Sergeant?"

"It would indeed, sir, because we do need those people to

be able to easily identify the sword and not have their recall impaired by seeing a dead body."

"We have a nice picture here, Colin, which people will enjoy looking at."

"Thanks, Dr. Crabtree, my compliments to the photographer."

With that, Knowles and Barnes left the lab and headed over to Manton Rempville Hall in Barnes' sleek white sports car, which Knowles thought would impress the upper-class individuals they were about to meet.

Chapter 2

Barnes drove down the carefully manicured driveway of Manton Rempville Hall, while Knowles stared at the yew hedges, which had been sheared into interesting shapes that he couldn't quite recognise. After they'd parked, Knowles walked over to one of the hedges and pointed.

"What do you think they're supposed to be, Barnesy, these shapes?"

Barnes looked at Knowles, who was moving his head around to try and get the right angle for a correct identification of the topiary.

"Well, Inspector, isn't that one a mouse and this one here a hedgehog?"

"It could be a hedgehog, I suppose, but I thought it might be a crouching lion – you see there's the mane and that's definitely a tail…"

"Excuse me, this is private property," said a very posh female voice, "if you don't leave I will call the police."

"Well, there's no need, because we are already here, madam," said Knowles, brandishing his identification card in the lady's face. "I am Detective Inspector Colin Knowles and this is Detective Sergeant Rod Barnes. We are here to ask you and your family about the death that occurred in the grounds of the monastery earlier today."

"Death, you say, is that why there were all those sirens keeping us awake at some ungodly hour this morning?"

"Those sirens were the ambulance and police cars rushing to the scene of a murder. I am sorry, but I don't know your name."

"The impertinence – I am Lady Bunny Johnson, if you must know, and why do those people put on their sirens when the murdered person is already dead and there's no reason to rush?" Lady Johnson smoothed her revealing blue blouse over her figure as she almost spat out these words.

"Thank you, Lady Johnson, I do need to know your name and there is always a reason to rush to a murder scene as vital evidence can easily be lost if the police aren't on the scene as soon as possible."

"Really – it doesn't seem necessary to me; perhaps they could put them on just in the afternoons?" She brushed a couple of blonde hairs behind her left ear, taking care not to get them caught in her silver earring, shaped like a unicorn.

"We'll see about that; anyway, how many people do you have in the Hall at the moment? I would like to interview them all, please."

"I'll ask the butler, Fairfax, to gather the staff together in the lower library for you."

"I would like to interview everyone in the house, staff, family, and house guests, if there are any of course."

"You surely can't believe that any members of the family, my family, would be involved in anything as sordid as a murder?"

"The murder was committed on a property adjacent to this Hall, last night, so I would like to eliminate every person in this Hall from my enquiries as soon as possible. So, Lady Johnson, if you please can you gather everyone in the library…"

"Which one, we have two? Upper or lower?"

"…please gather everyone in the lower library in fifteen minutes from now, so Sergeant Barnes and I can find out where everyone was last night."

"I'll ask Fairfax to gather the family and then he can go and get Wilkinson and Jenkins. I will ask Miss Newton to rouse everyone in the coach house."

With that Lady Johnson had gone, leaving behind a slight scent of neroli.

"I presume that's the coach house over there," said Barnes, pointing to a two-storey brick building behind some topiary bushes.

As if on cue, a youngish maid wearing an apron dashed

out of the front door of the Hall and headed in the direction of the building. Her auburn hair was in a bob, which swayed slightly as she hurried on her way.

"That must be Miss Newton doing as she has been bid by her boss," growled Knowles, "and I wonder who Wilkinson and Jenkins are?"

"They sound like a firm of undertakers to me," replied Barnes, "but presumably they're the gardeners or the chauffeurs or one of each."

Barnes' phone rang and he listened intently for around a minute, while Knowles tried to work out why anyone would shape a box hedge into the shape of a box. *These people have too much leisure time and too much money,*" he thought as Barnes finished his call and looked at him with a smile on his face.

"That was WPC Smythe – she has run some checks on Edward Pritchard and guess where he used to work?"

"He was a knife-grinder," said Knowles, not expecting to be right. He didn't like it when Barnes smiled at him; he felt like Barnes enjoyed knowing things that he didn't.

"He might have done something similar in his role as a sub-gardener here at Manton Rempville Hall."

"When did he stop working as a knife-grinding sub-gardener here at Manton Rempville Hall?" enquired Knowles.

"Three months ago, yesterday. He was dismissed because some money went missing from the house."

"Really, well I wonder whether he was ever given the opportunity to deny the allegations? I don't suppose we shall ever know, now that he's dead."

As he spoke, Miss Newton returned with two seventeen-year-old boys and a strikingly beautiful red-headed girl of about nineteen.

"Hello, I am Toby Johnson," said one of the boys, shaking Barnes by the hand.

Toby was around five feet nine inches tall and was wearing a worn T-shirt and jeans. His straight black hair was cut short. He continued, "This is my friend from Harrow, Basil Fawcett, and his amazing sister Henry. She's a stunner, isn't she? You must be the police who want to interview us."

"We are," said Knowles. "I am Inspector Knowles and this is Detective Sergeant Barnes."

"Anything of importance?" enquired Basil Fawcett, tossing his head slightly so that his brown hair fell in front of his eyes. He cleared it away from his glasses with the back of his left hand.

"It's very important, I can assure you," said Knowles, "and we will let you know in the fullness of time."

"Come on, Basil," said Henrietta Fawcett, "let's leave the policemen to their own devices and go in to the lower library. By the way, Sergeant Barnes, my real name is Henrietta, not Henry. If you'd like to make a note of that."

And with that the three walked into the Hall followed at an appropriate distance by Miss Newton. Barnes couldn't help noticing how Henrietta's red hair glinted in the faint sunlight.

Barnes had turned slightly red. Knowles looked at him and shook his head.

"Have you made a note, Sergeant?"

"No, sir, I haven't – I had realized she was a girl."

"I can tell, Sergeant Barnes, as I think she could too. Think of a nice ice-cold shower and you'll be fine."

"I wonder who this is?" said Barnes, pleased to be able to change the subject, "it's probably the gardener judging by his gloves."

"Afternoon, gentlemen. Are you the police who require my presence in the lower library?"

"Indeed we are, I am Sergeant Barnes and this is Inspector Knowles."

"Pleased to meet you both. I am the gardener, Jim Jenkins. I will see you in there in a few minutes; it'll take me an age to take my boots off." A slight grin split Jim Jenkins' ruddy complexion.

Suddenly, a slim, bearded man of average height came out of the house and started to march towards the two policemen. He completely ignored Jenkins, who stared at him in vain for some hope of recognition.

"Which one of you two oafs is in charge?"

13

"Neither of us is an oaf and I am the more senior officer. The name is Knowles, Detective Inspector Knowles, and this is my Detective Sergeant, Rod Barnes."

"Well, Inspector," said the man, drawing himself up to his full height of five feet seven inches, "I am a personal friend of the Chief Constable of this county and he will be hearing about your damned impertinence in suggesting that one of my family could be involved in someone's death. My name is Sir Michael Johnson."

"Sir Michael, please go to the lower library and let us explain everything to everyone when they are gathered together," suggested Knowles with all the tact he could muster.

"You do not tell me what to do in my own house. Let's get that clear."

"I am in charge of a murder investigation. I need to remove everyone in this house from my list of suspects. The best way to do this is to speak to you all at the same time initially and then take individual statements afterwards."

"I am going to complain to the Chief Constable about this method of interrogation you are employing."

"Don't complain too much, Sir Michael, it's Alan's, sorry the Chief Constable's, preferred method in these situations – one he recommended to me as a matter of fact."

Barnes looked surprised at this comment – he didn't think that Knowles knew the Chief Constable. Sir Michael looked taken aback and scratched his beard, slightly unsure of what to make of the comment.

"Let's get on with it then and see if it works - how long do we have to wait?"

"We will be there in a few minutes, I am just letting everyone gather together and settle down."

"I see, is that something the Chief Constable recommends too?"

"This part is optional. I will see you in a few minutes."

After Sir Michael had turned on his heel and gone back into the Hall, Barnes sidled over to Knowles and asked, "Do you really know the Chief Constable, sir?"

Knowles glanced around conspiratorially and straightened

his blue tie before saying, "I know who he is and I have attended the same gatherings as him on two occasions. I have met him and shaken his hand. I did also attend a course of his on group interrogations, during which he recommended a certain way of doing things. Namely, you break the news and then observe who looks at whom and whether anyone looks particularly blasé, which shows they are hearing news they already know."

"It's that straightforward, is it?"

"No, but it's worth a try, Barnesy. I will need you to watch for blasé looks and suspicious glances. Don't just stare at Henrietta with your tongue hanging out, watch everyone closely."

"Blasé looks and suspicious glances – understood, sir. Sounds like a plan. Shall we go in and find the lower library?"

"Yes, let's do that – this topiary is driving me batty."

The two men went through the front door and stood and admired the staircase, which was wooden with a central carpet of light red. To their left was an open door leading to a billiards or snooker room with the sound of voices beyond. The policemen walked past the snooker cues, card table and dartboard and looked through another doorway into the lower library, which had a circular staircase in the far corner. The chattering stopped and seventeen faces turned in expectation towards them.

"Ladies and gentlemen, thank you for gathering together at such short notice," began Knowles. "For those of you who don't know, I am Detective Inspector Colin Knowles and this is Detective Sergeant Rod Barnes. We are from Scoresby CID. I would appreciate it if everyone could provide their names one at a time starting from this side of the room," he gestured to his left, "so that when we interview you individually, we will know who we are talking to. Starting with you, sir."

As people said their names with varying degrees of irritation, Barnes noted down the name as well as their location within the room. Once all seventeen names had been provided Knowles continued.

"We are here in connection with a murder at the monastery last night at 11:06p.m. – the murder of a young man called Edward Pritchard." He paused to look around the room. "He was murdered by a person, or persons, unknown. He was stabbed through the back of the chest with a cavalry sword. My understanding is that Edward Pritchard was once employed here as a gardener."

There was a slight wave of consternation around the room and the policemen got the impression that everyone looked at someone different. Miss Newton put her head in her hands after looking at Gwendoline, who had glanced at her fiancé Ellis Hardaker, who had glared in the direction of James Beauregard, the friend of Cedric Johnson. Cedric was looking inquisitively at his mother, Bunny. Sir Michael Johnson spoke first.

"Edward Pritchard was sacked for gross misconduct – some money went missing from my study desk and he was seen acting suspiciously outside my study at roughly the time the money vanished. He denied it, of course, but he had to go. There were suspicions he was stealing plants from the gardens and selling them for profit to a local gardening centre."

"Did you call the police in over this matter, Sir Michael?" asked Barnes.

"We didn't, Sergeant, it was a family matter, and he had to go," replied Bunny Johnson. "He was causing problems for us as a family and it was better for all concerned that he leave immediately."

"Was he good at his job?" enquired Knowles.

"He was a hard worker, who could plant flowers and shrubs with great precision in a short time," replied Jenkins, "so, yes, he was good at his job. He mowed well and cut the hedges."

"He was also a thief and that was not part of his job, Inspector," said Sir Michael matter-of-factly.

"My next question relates to the sword that was used in the murder – it was a heavy cavalry sword dating from around 1796 as used by the Lifeguards, I believe. Do you have any such weapon missing from the house?"

Sir Michael enquired, "Do you have a picture, Inspector?"

Knowles handed him the picture taken by the Forensics photographer.

Sir Michael looked at the photo and nodded his head slightly. "Yes, the cavalry sword belonged to my great-great-great-grandfather and had been passed down to him from his own grandfather. It disappeared from the display cupboard in the upper library three months ago. Again, we didn't call the police as I assumed that someone within the house had taken it, perhaps even Edward Pritchard. It was the only item that was missing from the house."

"Is the cupboard normally locked?" asked Barnes.

"It normally is, but on this occasion the lock hadn't been turned properly and so whomever took it didn't have to use any force."

"I wonder where that sword has been in the past three months? It's not the sort of item that can be easily hidden away," continued Barnes.

"Perhaps the thief took it away from here when they left the premises, Sergeant," said Bunny Johnson with a hint of hopefulness in her voice.

"Why would someone come into your home and steal a sword from a display cabinet on the upper floor? That doesn't make any sense in my opinion," said Knowles. "How could a thief know it's there?"

"If they were collaborating with an ex-employee of my parents'," said Cedric Johnson, speaking for the first time.

"Edward would never have collaborated with another person to harm or hurt any one of us," said Gwendoline, "and it's a real insult to his memory to suggest otherwise, Cedric."

"Using all your naturally diplomacy as usual, Cedric," said Toby, winking at Sergeant Barnes, "you know that Gwendoline still holds a candle for Edward, even though Grandpa disapproved of her feelings for him and always did do. Not the right social class for his beloved granddaughter, eh Gramps?"

"Have more respect for your elders, Toby," hissed the grey-haired Gertrude Johnson at her grandson, "and never,

ever refer to your grandfather as Gramps again – don't they teach you any manners at Harrow these days?"

Gertrude was sitting with her stick in the comfiest chair in the room. George, her husband, appeared to be asleep by her side, though he had clearly spoken his name only a few moments earlier.

"Well, they teach us to think for ourselves, actually," said Basil Fawcett.

James Beauregard joined in. "Yes, Cedric, you are being extremely harsh on Edward; he was a very good-looking young man and could have been a model under different circumstances. He just needed some help; the ladies found him irresistible too, of course."

Henrietta Fawcett smiled at Sergeant Barnes and raised her eyebrows.

Sir Michael Johnson raised his hand as if to stop the chatter. "I am sure this family squabbling will only hinder the investigation of the police into this murder."

Knowles shook his head vigorously. "I disagree entirely, another ten minutes of that and we would have had our murderer identified."

"What are you talking about, man?" exclaimed Sir Michael.

"Edward Pritchard obviously arouses certain passions within certain people here, which could lead to murderous thoughts and, perhaps, murderous actions. I will need a statement from you all regarding your whereabouts between 10:00p.m. and midnight last night. If you can provide an alibi by citing an individual, or individuals, please do so."

"I thought you said the murder was committed at 11:06p.m., Inspector?" asked Timmy Beauregard, non-chalantly chewing his bubble gum.

Barnes smiled and looked at Knowles, who said, "My, someone was listening closely, weren't they - your whereabouts between 10:00p.m. and midnight; Sergeant, please hand out the statement forms and pens if necessary."

As Barnes handed around the forms, Knowles continued, "Once all the forms have been collected, we will need to read them and then perhaps interview you all, so we will need a private room for those interviews. Do you have somewhere suitable for these interviews to take place?"

"You can use the reading room in the coach house, Inspector Knowles. There's a couple of chairs and a desk, which should fit the bill nicely," said Lady Johnson. "Fairfax will take you over there once everyone has finished."

Knowles nodded appreciatively, but kept a careful eye on everyone, especially noting if someone's eyes were looking up and to the right, a sure sign of 'creativity' when writing a statement. Barnes on the other hand was looking at the women in the room, some more than others.

After a couple of minutes Knowles walked over to Barnes and blew in his ear.

"A word in your ear, Barnesy. Follow me for a moment."

"Certainly, sir."

They walked in to the sports room.

"Well, Sergeant, when I broke the news of Edward Pritchard's passing, what did you see?"

"I am going to draw this out on a large piece of paper when we get back to the station, but I saw James Beauregard look at Gwendoline, Henrietta looked at Gwendoline, as did Ellis Hardaker. Wilkinson, the chauffeur, looked at the cook, Mrs. Swarbrick, who was looking at Bunny Johnson, who looked straight ahead and seemed upset or shocked. Miss Newton looked at Toby, who was looking at George Johnson, as was his wife Gertrude. The butler, Fairfax, looked at Sir Michael who seemed to look out of the window and then glanced at Jenkins who had been looking at him. Cedric looked at his friend Timmy and then looked at George Johnson."

"Good observation, Sergeant, but some of those people could have been looking at someone else in their line of sight as everyone is close together in there."

"Possibly, but I got the impression those people were looking for one individual - what did you see, sir?"

"Basil Fawcett didn't look at anyone other than glancing at his sister and Gwendoline looked at her father, who didn't make eye contact."

"Who seemed the most upset?"

19

"To me, the lady of the house seemed the most shocked and didn't look at anybody. Gwendoline was surprised more than anything."

"Almost as though she'd seen Edward Pritchard recently, you mean?"

"Perhaps, yes, but I might be wrong of course."

'Did anyone appear pleased to you, sir?"

"Well, not joyous as such, but Ellis did manage a half-smile I thought."

"I thought Timmy Beauregard looked relieved…"

"Relieved?"

"Yes, sir, relieved, as though something was over for him."

"That's something to ask him later, indirectly of course, when we interview him."

"Overall I thought everyone took it very calmly indeed and there wasn't much chatter between people as there sometimes is; that was the most surprising part, not much chatter at all, as though very few people were surprised. Anyway, perhaps we should be getting back?"

"Yes, the butler has been trying to catch my attention for a few seconds...Mr. Fairfax, is there something you require?"

"Fairfax, sir, is my name…"

"You have been in service too long. Mr. Fairfax, are people ready to hand over their statements?"

"They are, Inspector; in which order should people come and be interviewed?"

"In the order they handed in their statements; you have some in your hand already, so let's get the others and we can begin the interviews."

Knowles gathered the remaining statements and decided to interview Gertrude Johnson first.

He explained to the assembled people, "I will interview Mrs. Johnson first - once our interview is finished I will then send for the next person; I would appreciate it if you remain in this room until all the interviews have been completed."

"But that could take ages," objected James Beauregard. "I have things to do and people to see, can I go next please?"

"I will see what I can do; I would like to eliminate you all from my enquiries, so leaving the premises won't allow me to do that, will it?"

"Mrs. Johnson, would you like some help walking over to the coach house?" asked Barnes in his kindest manner.

"No, thank you, young man, I still walk five miles per day on average, so I am sure I can totter over to the coach house."

"Right, well, I will see you over there then," said Barnes, knowing when he was not wanted. He looked up to see Henrietta looking at him admiringly. Barnes blushed slightly and hurriedly made his exit.

Knowles looked around the room to see who was talking to whom, but not much conversation was taking place. Bunny Johnson was looking out of the window and seemed to want to be on her own. The younger people were checking their emails or texting. Knowles wondered who was being told what, but decided he could do nothing about it and left the room.

Barnes had found the reading room and positioned two chairs on one side of the table and one on the other. He admired the blue and white striped wallpaper complementing the dark blue ceiling. There were some artificial flowers in a red vase on the piano. The low sun was bathing the room in a gentle light.

Knowles arrived just ahead of Mrs. Johnson and they sat down at the same time. He quickly read Mrs. Johnson's statement and handed it to Barnes. Knowles looked at the older woman and smiled.

"You were asleep between 10:00p.m. and midnight? Is that true? You didn't wake up at all?"

"I did wake up at some point during the night, to go to the toilet, but that was all. I think I heard someone outside our door, but I am not a hundred per cent sure."

"Which is your room?"

"Our bedroom is the one above the sports room, Inspector, where you saw the billiard table."

"Any idea of the time you heard someone outside your door?"

"None, Inspector, my husband blocks the fluorescent light

from the alarm clock with his glasses case and my watch is kept in the drawer. But wait, I heard the bells from St Anthony's church ringing briefly when I woke."

"Do they ring every hour?"

"I think this was practice, not keeping time." Gertrude nodded her head gently as if to reassure herself she was right.

"We will find out what time they finished last night."

"Any idea which way the person outside your room was heading?" asked Barnes.

"Down the stairs, I think, as I heard their footfalls for a few seconds."

"Were the footfalls heavy or light, would you say?"

"They were light steps I think, but it could just have been someone being considerate knowing we were asleep rather than someone trying to avoid detection."

'Of course, that's the most likely explanation. Who would have walked by your door? What are the other rooms on that side of the house?"

"Well, there's the upper library and my son's bedroom."

"So it was most likely Sir Michael or Bunny then?'

"Or anyone coming out of the upper library," interjected Knowles.

"Where the sword was kept before it was stolen," said Barnes.

"The sword was stolen a while ago," objected Mrs. Johnson, raising her hand to her temple and rubbing it gently.

"Yes, but it might not have been moved very far, Mrs. Johnson, not stolen as much as relocated in the library for future use. If it were found, then the thief or relocator would not have been incriminated." Barnes leaned forward so both his arms were resting on the table.

"I see – well, that implies a lot of forward planning on behalf of the thief or relocator as you call them. As though they were imagining using the sword for the crime that was committed last night."

"Indeed, Mrs. Johnson, this killer is rather cold-blooded in their planning, as though they were anticipating Edward Pritchard returning and they already knew, ahead of time, how they were going to deal with him."

"You believe that Edward Pritchard was blackmailing the killer?"

Knowles interrupted the conversation. "Well, we have no firm ideas yet, so I think we have used up enough of your time for now, Mrs. Johnson. Could you please ask Wilkinson, the chauffeur, to come and see us next?"

Mrs. Johnson nodded her consent, rose from the table, and bade the policemen a fond farewell.

"Could she could have heard the killer heading down the stairs, do you think, sir?" asked Barnes.

"Well, Barnesy, I doubt it unless the killer is a bit of a Jekyll and Hyde character - clever enough to hide a sword in a library and plan the murder, yet stupid enough to walk past people's bedrooms holding that sword. I think the killer is clever and smart enough to use the circular staircase to go downstairs and thus reduce the chances of being seen and heard. When these interviews are over let's go to St Anthony's in Manton Rempville village and see if we can find out when those bell ringers were practicing their peals and rounds last night."

"What did Wilkinson say in his statement?"

"Let's just read it together, Sergeant."

As Knowles and Barnes finished reading the three sentences of the statement the chauffeur appeared in the doorway.

"Please sit down, Mr. Wilkinson," said Barnes.

"Thank you, sir." Wilkinson eased his six foot frame into the chair.

"Do you have a first name, Mr. Wilkinson?"

"I do, Sergeant, it's Barry."

"Well, Barry, you say in your statement that you were at home with your wife between 10:00p.m. and midnight last night - can she verify that?"

"She can provide an alibi, if that's what you mean."

"What's your wife's name and where is it you live exactly?"

"She's called Muriel and we live in an estate house in the village."

"Manton Rempville?"

23

"Yes, close by, should anyone need a lift at a moment's notice." Wilkinson grinned and winked at Knowles.

"Are you on call at all times, then?"

"Theoretically, but really it's just between 8:00a.m. and 6:00p.m. most days, although I have had to pick up Cedric and Toby late at night from various pubs in the area."

"Boys will be boys, eh?"

"Indeed they will, Sergeant."

"I think that's everything for the moment, Barry," said Knowles. "Could you write your address on this statement so we can check your alibi?"

As Barry Wilkinson wrote his address, Knowles asked him to tell Ellis Hardaker that he was the next person to be interviewed.

Once Wilkinson had left the room, Knowles handed Hardaker's statement to Barnes and then phoned WPC Smythe at Scoresby station.

"Hello, Linda, did I wake you up?... Sorry - could you go to 3 Hall Street in Manton Rempville and interview Muriel Wilkinson regarding her husband's activities last night? He claims he was at home with her. Yes. If she could corroborate that statement I'd appreciate it. Thanks."

Ellis Hardaker strode into the room without introduction and sat down in the chair. His black hair and moustache were neatly trimmed and he was wearing slacks and a purple polo shirt. He fixed his green eyes upon the Inspector.

"I do hope this isn't going to take very long, Inspector Knowles."

"We'll see what we can do. Your statement indicates you went out to dinner with Gwendoline and returned to the Hall around 11:10p.m. then went to bed at once."

"Precisely, that's what I wrote and that's what happened."

"You both went to bed at the same time?"

"Gwendoline had a shower and then I had one after her."

"You didn't shower together, then?"

"No we didn't - when I got to our bedroom I realised I had left something in the car and went downstairs to get it."

"Did anyone see you, Mr. Hardaker?"

"They may have, but I didn't see anyone."

24

"What was it you left in your car, Mr. Hardaker?"

"My i-Pad - I needed to send an e-mail to a business associate."

"And did you send that e-mail from the car or from the room?"

"From the car - there's an open wireless network here at the Hall, so I used that."

Knowles looked impressed, but Barnes made a mental note to check this statement.

Barnes continued with the questioning, noting that Ellis had folded his arms across his chest...

"When the Inspector here announced Edward Pritchard's death I was watching you and I thought I saw a half-smile cross your lips, before you looked at Gwendoline who didn't look back at you at all."

"Well, Gwendoline had a crush on the sub-gardener if you must know; almost like a teenager has on a good-looking film star, but it had passed, I can assure you. As for the smile, well that's probably because I wasn't surprised. He'd upset a lot of people by snooping around watching people in their private affairs."

"Gwendoline was over him, you think?"

"I am a hundred per cent sure of it, Sergeant."

"Which is your bedroom?"

"The north-east bedroom; the one that looks over towards the monastery."

"Did you see any lights in that direction?"

"I didn't look out of the window, so I can't answer."

"Did you hear any bells from the church?"

"Bells, no I can't remember hearing any bells, but then again we are on the wrong side of the house to hear the bells from St Anthony's. The church is to the west of here." Ellis Hardaker helpfully pointed in the direction of Manton Rempville.

"I see - well I have no more questions for now, please can you send in Basil Fawcett next? Thank you, Mr. Hardaker."

Mr. Hardaker nodded his assent and left the room as quickly as he'd arrived.

"What do you reckon about the bells, Barnesy?"

"Practice finished before 11:15p.m., which is a relief for the locals I am sure."

"Indeed - let's see what Basil has to say for himself. According to this statement, he and Henrietta only arrived yesterday afternoon from London, so they were just getting used to the surroundings, i.e. the local pub."

"I wonder which pub that would be?"

"White Hart in Norton-juxta-Wychwood, probably, the best pub in the area according to CAMRA for the real ale."

Barnes was playing with his mobile phone trying to find the wireless network that Ellis Hardaker had referred to, but couldn't find one without a password.

"Ellis must have known the password to the local network as I can't find anything without one."

Suddenly, Knowles put his finger to his lips and pointed to the door. "There's someone outside," he mouthed to Barnes and pointed. Barnes stood up and walked quietly to the doorway - he stood by the frame for about five seconds and then leapt out. Basil Fawcett jumped slightly but managed to maintain his calm demeanour.

"What were you hoping to hear, Basil?" asked Barnes after he'd escorted the young man into the room.

"Well some of us think that Ellis Hardaker must have been the murderer and so I thought I would listen to your post-interview discussion to see whether you did too."

Knowles looked upset. "You've been texting each other about this? Who started it?"

"I am sure it was Timmy Beauregard who sent a message to Cedric - he forwarded it to Toby, who passed it to Henrietta and myself." Basil adjusted his glasses nervously.

"Why is Timmy Beauregard so keen to implicate Ellis in the murder?"

"I am not sure - perhaps he has designs on Gwendoline?"

"Mmmm - interesting theory, Basil, anyway which pub did you visit last night?"

"The White Lion in Stoney Stafford and then the White Hart in Norton something or other."

Knowles put two thumbs up and winked at Barnes who shook his head in mock sadness.

"Good choices, especially the second one. How did you get to Norton something or other, Basil?"

"Taxis, Inspector. We got back around 11:30p.m. and I headed to bed here in the coach house - I was a bit tired after travelling up from London."

"Was anyone else around?"

"There was someone standing outside the study windows I thought, but it might have been one of the statues - I'd had three pints of bitter and a couple of whiskies during the evening."

"Enough to see a few people perhaps," chortled Knowles, "which bitter did you have?"

"A pint of Pedigree and a couple of Norfolk Wherrys plus two doubles of Laphroaig."

"Another good choice, but I prefer Bruichladdich myself."

"That's unpeated isn't it," said Basil, "I haven't tried that one yet."

"There's plenty of time for you yet," said Knowles, "and it will be worth the wait. Anyhow, who was with you last night?"

"Henry, or Henrietta I suppose I should say, and Toby, of course, plus we met a couple of his friends, James and George Flavell, at the Hart. They both spent the evening staring at Henrietta of course. I am sure you can appreciate why." Fawcett spoke this last sentence while looking at Barnes, who reddened slightly.

"So Toby and Henrietta will have the same story as you by the time they come here to be interviewed, will they?"

"I would doubt that, Inspector, They went for a walk together after I went to bed, so I am sure they'll be able to come up with more suspects for you than I have."

"Did you hear any bells, last night, Basil?" asked Barnes.

"You mean church bells, I presume? Well let me think...you know I am sure I did at some point, when we were getting out at The Hart in Norton..."

"Norton-juxta-Wychwood?"

"That's the one."

"And that would have been around what time?"

"Around 10 I suppose, not much after."

"I see. Any idea which church they were from?"

"None whatsoever. This is only my second visit to the area, so I don't know my way around yet."

"When the news of the death was announced, you didn't show any emotion and you didn't look at anyone at all - why was that?"

"Well, I never did meet Edward Pritchard face-to-face, but I have heard some stories about him. He seemed to be at the centre of a number of problems. A number of the ladies seemed to dote on him, especially Lady Johnson." Basil moved his fringe from in front of his eyes.

"Is that why she's so upset at his loss?"

"I wasn't aware she was, Sergeant, although she seemed to be staring out of the window when I left, so you might be correct that she's upset."

"How do you know the ladies doted on him, Basil?"

"Both Henry and I were here about three months ago and Edward Pritchard was still employed here then. You could tell Gwendoline was in awe of him as was Miss Newton, the maid, and the cook, Mrs. Swarbrick."

"Did you mind the ladies doting on him - would you have preferred to be the centre of attention?"

"Oh, no thank you, I have a nice, quiet girlfriend."

"Who else was here when you were three months ago?"

"The same crowd, apart from Timmy Beauregard. Even Mr. Johnson's parents were here."

"There's a coincidence," said Knowles. "I wonder who invited everyone back and why?"

"I was happy to be back, myself. It's a great place to come for the weekend."

"One final thing, Basil, were you in the monastery grounds this morning? A witness has told us that she saw three younger people horsing around and playing at sword fighting. Was that you and Toby and Henrietta?"

"It was us I am afraid - the sword fighting sounds in poor taste, but we didn't know at the time about the murder."

"Thank you for the information, Basil, can you ask Timmy Beauregard to come and see us next, please? And please leave straightaway rather than hanging around outside the door where your reflection can be seen in the window pane."

"Oh, that's how you knew I was there."

"Indeed, Basil."

"Right, I'll go." Basil left rather sheepishly.

"So, Sergeant Barnes, what do you reckon about what young Basil said?"

"Young Basil was very interesting, sir, because he heard some bells and he has been here previously at the same time as everyone else by the sound of it."

"Why would you invite exactly the same crowd as three months previously, unless you were trying to correct something that had happened at the previous gathering? Set the record straight, perhaps, put things right - do you know what I mean?"

"You mean murder Edward Pritchard to right a slight suffered three months previously in front of everyone who was there at that time?"

"It's possible, almost probable, perhaps, but who would invite everyone here?"

"It could only be Sir Michael or his wife, Bunny."

"That's what you'd think, but if Bunny is suggestible then it could have been someone else."

"Even Edward Pritchard?"

"If she doted on him then by all means, but why would he do that?"

"So he could clear his name in front of all the guests, prove himself innocent of the reasons why he was sacked."

"And then someone else found out what he was up to and killed him to silence him?"

"That sounds incredibly plausible all of a sudden."

There was a cough from the doorway, where the slim figure of Timmy Beauregard was standing.

"Come in, Timmy, and sit yourself down," said Knowles, looking at the university student whose slight acne made him look younger than he was. Timmy smiled and smoothed his expensive trousers.

"So, Timmy, where were you last night between 10 and midnight?" asked Barnes.

Timmy ran his fingers through his ginger hair as he replied.

"Well, at 11:06 I was with my brother and Cedric at the Badger and Ferret in Goat Parva. We were in the pub from 9:30p.m. onwards and came back around 11:30."

"Did you hear any bells, Timmy, when you were out and about last night?"

"That's an interesting question...I can't say that I did, but I've lived near churches all my life, so I just might be tuning them out."

"When you returned, was there anyone around?"

"I don't think I saw anyone; I heard an owl over by the monastery but that was all - it's so very quiet here, you know, a great place for watching birds though I haven't had much of a chance to use my binoculars yet. Miss Newton likes watching the birds too apparently, especially the owls at the monastery."

"I see - she doesn't strike me as the type - this is the first time you've been here, Timmy?"

"It is, Inspector. I was invited three months ago, but I was ill and didn't feel like attending the weekend, so I declined at the last minute."

"Who invited you this time?"

"Cedric did, but he told me that his mother was the one who wanted to get everyone back together again."

Barnes and Knowles looked at each other and smiled.

Knowles continued, "When James came back from the previous gathering did he mention anything about what had happened?"

"Well, Inspector, James is gay and he was enthralled by Edward Pritchard, but I believe the feelings weren't reciprocated as Pritchard was literally into someone else."

"Who, Gwendoline?" blurted Barnes, smiling.

Timmy laughed and wagged his finger at Barnes.

"James didn't think so. He didn't have definite proof, but he had his suspicions about the lady of the house - she's called Bunny for a reason, apparently."

"That would explain why she's apparently upset and staring out of the window," said Barnes, winking at Knowles.

"If that was the case, why would she invite everyone back again, Timmy?"

"I would presume she'd enjoyed everyone's company the first time around and wanted us all back. Or...perhaps she thought that something had started three months ago and would either continue or be completed in this gathering?"

"Why do you say that, Timmy?"

"No particular reason, Inspector. It's just that James told me last time he felt as though there was something going on in the background, but he couldn't work out what."

"Well, we'll be sure to ask him what the something was. One final thing, Timmy. Why did you look relieved when you heard Pritchard was dead?"

Timmy bit his lip before replying.

"I probably did because James was hit really very hard when Pritchard rejected him. He doesn't take these things well and it takes him ages to recover."

"I see, you were relieved for your brother and we will respect that."

"Thank you. Who should I tell to come and see you next?"

"Please ask Mrs. Swarbrick to come over and see us."

"I will do as you ask. Thank you for listening to me."

"It was a pleasure, Timmy."

After Timmy Beauregard had left, Knowles looked at Barnes and asked, "What did you make of that, Sergeant?"

"An exceedingly bright boy, who might just see and notice too much for his own good one day. I have never had anyone thank me for listening to them before - isn't that a bit unusual, sir?"

"It is, Sergeant, and shows a rare sensitivity, because we were listening to him very carefully and he obviously picked up on that. He heard no bells, either, but as he said himself that doesn't mean there weren't any."

"I wonder why he was invited when he didn't attend the first gathering three months ago?"

"Perhaps the brothers are inseparable or maybe James was worried something might happen and made sure brother Timmy came along this time?"

"Why would James accept an invitation to a weekend party if he felt threatened and needed his brother to be there for some kind of protection?"

"Because he was fascinated by something or someone and he wanted to find out what the possibilities might be?"

"He might have been infatuated with Edward Pritchard?"

"Can I come in?" said a stocky, ginger-haired figure at the door. Knowles and Barnes both looked at the forty-something woman with slight surprise as neither of them had heard her arrive.

"Mrs. Swarbrick - you have been very quick to get over here; did you run?"

"No, Inspector, you collected my statement after Timmy Beauregard's so I thought I might be next, so I came over here just after he left."

"That is very astute of you, Mrs. Swarbrick, do sit down. How is lunch coming along for your house guests?"

"You were right about James Beauregard in what you were saying; he couldn't take his eyes off Edward Pritchard; Edward was working in the kitchen gardens once and James was in the kitchen just staring at him and getting in my way in the process. Lunch is coming along nicely thank you - to answer your question."

"Thank you for the information, Mrs. Swarbrick…"

"Please call me Elspeth."

"Elspeth…are you aware whether James' was an unrequited love?"

"I am sure it was. James had never seen Edward before."

"This was three months ago?"

"Yes, James had never been here before and he fell in love with Edward I am sure. He didn't hide his feelings - everyone would have been aware of how he felt, but I doubt they even spoke you know, as Gwendoline and Henrietta were always in the way."

"Henrietta?" said Barnes, looking disappointed.

"And Mrs. Johnson, of course. She was always watching and hoping too, I suspect."

"Hoping for what?" said Knowles.

"Hoping for a piece of the action, as it were." Mrs.

Swarbrick's florid complexion reddened even more under her cook's hat as she spoke unkindly about her employer.

"She had fallen for him too?"

"Not necessarily, but she is rather short of fun in her life." Mrs. Swarbrick readjusted her position in the chair.

"I see, so any port in a storm?"

"That sort of thing, Inspector."

"Is that why he was sacked by Sir Michael?"

"I think not just for that reason - he was accused of stealing plants, but I am sure that was Jim Jenkins who framed him. I believe that Edward also tried to blackmail Miss Newton, who he said was having an affair with Cedric. She told me as much and there was no truth in it at all."

"He wasn't trying to ingratiate himself with people, was he?"

"He was charming and he noticed things going on around him that he could twist to his advantage."

"So where were you last night, Elspeth? According to your statement you fell asleep in a chair in the kitchen and then headed over to your cottage around 11:00p.m. Can anyone verify this for you?"

"No, my husband's away on the rigs right now and I don't recall seeing anyone around when I headed over to the village."

"Your cottage is in Manton too, like Mr. Wilkinson?"

"That's right, Inspector, we live in the same row of estate cottages."

"Was he in last night?"

"The lights were on, I seem to remember."

"And no one saw you?"

"Not that I noticed."

"Did you hear any bells or an owl hoot over by the monastery?" asked Barnes.

"There's always owls over in that direction," replied Mrs. Swarbrick, "and as for the bells, I did hear some bells ringing when I was leaving the Hall, but they stopped and then later I heard the clock ring the quarter hour."

"This was from St Anthony's church?"

"It's the nearest church, so I presume so."

"You say there's always owls in that direction - do they nest over there in the ruins?" enquired Knowles.

"I think they must, Inspector - I only ever hear them and never see them."

"Did you ever speak to Edward Pritchard yourself?"

"Very rarely, Sergeant, he was always outside and even ate his sandwiches out there."

"So where did he live?"

"He rented a room in Jenkins' cottage in the village - Jim isn't married so there was room for Edward too."

"So when he was sacked then he would have lost his room as well?"

"Officially that is true, but Jim didn't throw Edward out straightaway; he let him find another place first."

"That was kind of him, given that Edward was stealing plants from the gardens."

"Well, if you want to know what I think about that - Edward was framed and Jim was the one taking the plants and selling them to other people." Mrs. Swarbrick's hand went to adjust the ginger hair that was peeking out from under her hat.

"Edward was fired for a few reasons then?"

"Yes, stealing plants, taking money, being attractive to the daughter of the house and other people too."

"Right, well, I think we've taken up enough of your valuable time, Elspeth, so could you ask Sir Michael Johnson to come and see us?"

"Not Toby?"

"Why do you ask?"

"You collected his statement after mine."

"Well, that might be, but I do like to change things sometimes. Thank you, Elspeth,"

Mrs. Swarbrick stood up and flattened down her skirt, before heading out of the room.

"So, the Lord of the Manor next," said Barnes, "are you going to ask him about his wife and Edward, sir?"

"Not in so many words," smiled Knowles, "but his answer might have an important bearing on the case."

"Are you any closer to knowing what happened?"

"I don't have a clue what actually happened, but I think you will find almost all the people we interview will have had a reason to kill Edward."

"Even Henrietta?"

"I think so, Sergeant, she probably fell for him and found out later that he didn't have any feelings for her."

"How could he lead her on like that?"

"Practice, Barnesy, plenty of practice...oh, here we are."

Sir Michael Johnson appeared and wagged his finger at Knowles.

"How dare you use a member of my staff to summon me, Sir Michael Johnson, to your presence in my own house?"

"It was just the order the statements were gathered in," said Knowles, not entirely convincingly. Barnes yawned instead of smiling.

Sir Michael glowered at Knowles; the creases in the knight of the realm's forehead were emphasized because of the paleness of his skin.

"I was out with my constituency agent last night talking about our plans for the next election when I will be running as the Conservative candidate."

"And you returned to the house at around 11:30p.m. having driven from his house in Stoney Stafford?"

"That's correct - at 11:30p.m. precisely."

"That would have taken you very close to the monastery, wouldn't it?"

"It would and it did and I didn't see a thing."

"Did you hear any owls or bells?" enquired Barnes.

"I didn't, Sergeant Barnes - but then I wouldn't hear anything as I was playing my Scarlatti CD in the car."

"And when you returned home, was there anyone else around?"

"I didn't see anyone."

"Did you see a statue outside the study window?"

Sir Michael pointed in the direction of the study. "There's no statue outside that window, what kind of question is that?" He leaned forwards in his chair, daring the officers.

"A fair one, given that someone else saw a statue there last night."

"No statue has ever been situated there since I have lived here."

"So why would someone stand outside the study window at that time of night?"

"I have no idea. Perhaps they were getting a breath of fresh air?" Sir Michael was not containing his exasperation very well.

"Or looking out towards the monastery waiting for a sign?"

"Well, they weren't there when I came home."

"Why did you sack Edward Pritchard, Sir Michael?"

Sir Michael sat up straight and stroked his beard. He then counted out the reasons on his left hand.

"He stole money from me, he flirted with my daughter who was already spoken for, he stole plants from my garden, he didn't do his work correctly - that's all I can think of at the moment, but I think that's more than enough."

"He didn't do his work correctly. What does that mean?"

"His topiary skills were crude beyond measure; suffice to say he claimed one of the bushes was a unicorn and I didn't believe him - the horn was pointing straight at my daughter's bedroom. Suggestive and rude."

"Sounds more interesting than the box topiary at the front."

"That is ironical gardening, Inspector, created from box trees."

"I see, well the irony was lost on me, Sir Michael."

"Evidently." Sir Michael shook his head.

"When was the last time you saw Edward Pritchard, Sir Michael?"

"Three months ago when he left our house for the last time."

"You haven't seen him since?"

"No, what reason would I have?"

"He might have come back to see Gwendoline?"

"If he'd come back to see Gwennie, the last person on earth he would want to see would be me. Besides, if he had been here Fairfax would have told me."

"He'd tell you everything, would he?"

"He would; he's my faithful retainer."

Knowles looked at Barnes who shook his head.

"Well, Sir Michael, I think that's everything for now. Would you kindly ask Toby to come and see us next? Thank you."

After Sir Michael had left, Barnes smiled broadly.

"A topiary unicorn, how likely is that? No one would do that unless they were wanting to be sacked, would they?"

"Exactly. He was framed again, I presume, because as you say no one is that idiotic."

"How would you prove that you hadn't sculpted a piece of topiary?"

"I don't think you can, especially if you can't provide an alibi for your exact whereabouts."

"Or you could, sir, but doing so would get you into even more trouble."

"And get someone else into trouble too."

"I wonder who that would be; presumably someone connected with that other person and who wanted revenge on Edward Pritchard would organise the sculpting."

"I wonder what time of day you would sculpt a topiary unicorn so that no one else would notice and how long it would take?"

"Good questions, Inspector - we should ask Jenkins - but why would you admit you had done something when you hadn't in fact done that something?"

"Perhaps Pritchard didn't admit it? Perhaps he was close to the topiary when Sir Michael saw him and Sir Michael jumped to the incorrect conclusion."

"Are you getting the impression that Edward Pritchard wasn't the sharpest knife in the box?"

"Yes, definitely, anyway young Toby's here by the sound of it."

The outside door had been closed and soon Toby Johnson appeared.

"Toby, do come in and sit down."

"Thank you, Inspector." Toby lolled in the chair with his legs splayed, showing off the designer cuts in his jeans to perfection.

37

"So your statement concurs with Basil Fawcett's, more or less."

"It would do as we were together most of the evening except that Henry, sorry Henrietta, and I went for a walk after we returned to clear some of the fog out of our heads."

"Did you have much to drink then?"

"No, about three pints and a couple of chasers, but that was about it."

"What did you have?"

"I had mostly Marstons - Pedigree and one pint of another beer; I am not that good with the names of the beers - I know the taste of the ones I like though." Toby smiled.

"And how long was your walk with Henrietta?"

"It was around half-an-hour, forty minutes, that sort of thing - we walked around the perimeter of the property and over to the monastery."

"Did you see anyone else?"

"Well, I thought I did. When we were walking towards the monastery; I thought I saw two people standing close to one another, but when we came out of the trees they had gone."

Knowles leaned forward.

"Which part of the monastery were those two people standing in?"

"They were in the north transept I think; highlighted by the moonlight for a few seconds."

"Did the figures remind you of anyone? Could one of them have been Edward Pritchard?"

"They were androgynous, similar height, similar build, but who they were I don't know." Toby shrugged his shoulders.

"Did you walk across the refectory?"

"Yes, we did."

"Any signs of a struggle or a quarrel?"

"We didn't see anything untoward, but there could have been someone in the shadows and we wouldn't have seen anything."

"Presumably, you weren't looking at the ground for much of the time?" asked Barnes.

"No, Sergeant, Henrietta is very arresting, especially in the moonlight."

Barnes smiled at Toby's little joke.

"I'll bet she is. If those two people you saw at the monastery had come from this house would you have seen them on your way back?"

"Not necessarily, we came back the southern way; they could have gone the northern way and so stayed in the trees the whole time. They might have used the secret passage too, but that's risky because you can't unlock it from the outside."

"What secret passage would that be, Toby?" asked Knowles askance. Barnes' eyes had lit up with delight on hearing of the underground escape route.

"No one has mentioned that then, right, well it runs from the southern wall in the lounge towards the monastery and comes out near the outer wall. The secret passage was an escape route for priests in the time of religious persecution around 1600 - it was one of the last ones to be constructed by Nicholas Owen before he was tortured after the Gunpowder Plot."

"We will have to examine this passage afterwards - how does it work?"

"It starts as a recess behind the books, the door for which is locked by a switch behind a lamp - if that's locked you can't unlock the door from within the passage, so you are stuck until it's unlocked."

"But you could go down the passage and leave the door unlocked and then come back again and still re-enter the Hall?"

"Got it in one, Inspector."

"Is it normally left locked?"

"I would hope so, Inspector, although not too many people in the local villages know about the passage of course."

"How do you mean - not too many?"

"Well, the staff are supposed to keep it a secret, but I believe Edward Pritchard told a few of his friends about the passage and that's almost certainly how the money came to be stolen from my father's study."

"How do you know he did that?"

"The barmaid at The Hart in Norton-juxta-Wychwood told me - her name is Erin Beard, we call her Beardy, and she told me that Pritchard got drunk one evening and told her about the passage in a loud voice, so half the people in the pub could hear."

"Was there a move to block the passage after this event?"

"No - the door at the monastery is well hidden in a bank under some bushes, so making it more secure would only make it more obvious, if you see what I mean."

"I meant locking the door from the inside at the monastery end."

"It's not lockable because there's no lock; it's a trapdoor covered with soil - I will show you if you like, once you've interviewed everyone of course."

"Thank you, Toby. Sergeant Barnes will gladly take you up on that offer in half-an-hour or so."

Barnes nodded and smiled; he'd been hoping that there'd be a secret passage since arriving at the Hall. He felt the murderer must have used the passage as there seemed to have been a lot of people around the Hall late at night, none of whom had seen a person carrying a sword.

"Did you walk past the trapdoor last night, Toby?"

"No, Sergeant, we weren't within thirty yards of it, so we couldn't see whether it had been used recently."

"Fair enough; so, Toby, I think that's all for now. Could you ask George Johnson to come and see us please?"

"Old Gramps, I will certainly do that; Grandma will probably accompany him to the front door as he's not so good on his legs any longer."

"Thank you, Toby."

After Toby had left Knowles put his head in his hands and rubbed his face quite briskly.

"Barnesy, when do you think they were planning on telling us about the secret passage - when exactly? A vital piece of information that we're told about in an offhand moment by the youngest member of the household."

"Perhaps they thought we knew about it already?"

"Not likely, which shows that perhaps not so many people

know about the secret passage after all. We should interview Erin Beardy or whatever her name is after we've finished."

"Haven't we had dealings with her before? Something to do with illegally importing cigarettes?"

"Yes, she claimed that she smoked five thousand ciggies on a monthly basis."

"A hundred and seventy per day - that's right - one every six minutes of every waking moment of every single day."

"It seems like everyone we have spoken to was around the Hall at some time between 10 and midnight and yet nobody has been able to positively identify another person."

"It's a bit like Murder on the Orient Express, except there's only one stab wound."

"With the sword still in it."

"Could the sword have been left in the secret passage?"

"You should check for possible hiding places in the secret passage. It would certainly help the murderer if the sword had been hidden - no awkward questions about three foot long pieces of metal being concealed about the person."

"I think I hear George heading this way."

The tapping of a stick on the stone floor could be heard down the passageway. Eventually George Johnson pottered into the room and semi-collapsed into the chair opposite Knowles and Barnes.

"Hello officers, I am not as fit as I once was I am afraid." George laughed at his own joke as he had never felt very fit in his entire life.

"Take your time, Mr. Johnson, just compose yourself for a few seconds." Knowles tried to sound reassuring.

"Right, I thank you for that thought, but I will be fine so let's commence with the interview."

"You say that you and your wife went to bed quite early, around 10:00p.m., and that you fell asleep straightaway and didn't wake up until around 4:00a.m."

"That's more or less it, very boring I'm afraid, sorry I can't be of any more interest." He scratched his ear in a distracted manner.

"Did you hear any bells or owls hooting or any activity in the direction of the monastery?" asked Barnes.

"There were some bells ringing when we came to bed; I presume they were from St Anthony's and that they were practicing for a service. As for the owls, I hear them every time we go to bed - the hoots come from the direction of the monastery. I think they must nest in the ruins. As for activity over by the monastery, well I did look over in that direction, but we don't have much of a view that way - we can only see the bushes on the south side. However, I did think I saw someone hanging around those bushes at one point."

"What time was this?"

"Roughly 10:15p.m."

"I wonder who that could have been? Most people we've interviewed weren't around at that time."

"Perhaps it was Edward Pritchard skulking around the ruins?"

"Waiting to meet someone from the Hall, you mean?"

"Almost certainly." George nodded at his own words; he was convinced he was right.

"Who would that be, do you think?"

"I've no idea, Inspector, perhaps one of the servants?"

"Don't they all have their own homes where they could meet Edward Pritchard?"

"They do, but perhaps their significant other was around and might overhear something?"

"So, they could meet in a pub then, not in a windy, exposed monastery."

"Not if they intended to murder him."

"And who would want to do that, George?" asked Knowles quite innocently.

"I am sure I have no idea; I am just throwing ideas around."

"People who throw things usually have a target."

"Purely hypothetical postulates, nothing concrete of course."

"Right, of course, well, I think we have taken up enough of your time George - could you please ask Mr. Jenkins to come and see us? Thank you."

"So, you were following what I was saying. I was beginning to think you'd not understood." He ran his fingers through his thinning hair with something approaching relief.

"His was the statement I collected after yours, George,'" said Knowles.

"Of course," said George, tapping the side of his nose with his finger, "of course, that's the reason." He then rose on unsteady legs and headed out of the room.

"Trying to protect the family by suggesting that only the staff could have wanted to murder Edward Pritchard - a thinly veiled collective character assassination if ever I heard one," said Barnes after a few seconds of silence.

"Why would Jenkins want to murder Pritchard, anyway? Jenkins has no significant other," wondered Knowles.

"Perhaps he acquired one after Pritchard left?"

"We should ask him, unless George was inferring that Jenkins would have been entertaining someone for the evening?"

"In that case he's not likely to pop out for a quick murder at the monastery, is he?"

"So what was he getting at?"

"Staff in general, perhaps, or perhaps staff we haven't yet interviewed, such as Fairfax or Miss Newton - not just Jenkins?"

"Fairfax is the butler and so would be normally beyond reproach, so that really leaves only Miss Newton. She doesn't strike me as having hidden secrets that George would find out about."

"Perhaps George has been hearing rumours from his family."

"There's always that, Barnesy...hark, I hear the sound of boots approaching."

A few seconds later Jenkins the gardener was occupying the seat opposite them. He'd offered to take his boots off, but the police had told him to keep them on.

Barnes asked the first question:

"It's Jim, isn't it?"

"Yes, Sergeant." Jenkins smiled with relief; he'd been expecting a tougher question.

"Jim, how long is it since Edward Pritchard moved out of your house?"

43

"About a month - he moved to a rented house in the village."

"So you live on your own, then?"

"Apart from the cat, yes, I do."

"Right, so if someone was under the impression that you had a significant other then they'd be mistaken?"

"They'd be dead wrong, Sergeant Barnes." Jenkins shook his head with some sadness.

"Right, well, that's cleared that up then."

"Yes, it appears to have although I was always certain that I was living on my own."

"Apart from the cat," said Knowles. "What's the cat's name?"

"Albert - he's a five-year-old tabby cat, good mouser when he can be bothered."

"It's a difficult age for cats," replied Knowles, "they're in their late thirties in human terms, so are just looking around for a role in life."

"Albert's role is to sleep on the kitchen window sill then," said Jenkins, chuckling, "and he's practicing long and hard."

Barnes looked at Knowles to see whether the cat conversation was going to carry on and when he saw that it had finished, he continued.

"You say in your statement that you were at home the whole evening; can anyone verify that?"

"Nobody can because I didn't see anyone; oh, but I did go down to the Red Lion in the village for a quick pint around 10:15p.m., so I suppose the barman, Syd Watt, would remember me, if you were to ask him."

"We will ask him, Jim, trust us on that."

"Right, I wasn't away for more than twenty minutes though."

"Understood - how did Sir Michael find out that Edward Pritchard was stealing plants?"

Jim Jenkins shifted uneasily in his chair and rubbed his light brown hair.

"Well, I voiced my concerns to Sir Michael directly, as the number of plants delivered was roughly twice as many as were being planted by my estimates."

"Did you confront Edward about this?"

"I did and he told me a lot of them were diseased and had to be disposed of in a fire. I told him that we should report that to the wholesaler as it was in breach of their agreement with us and so he said he would do that."

"And did he contact the wholesaler?"

Jenkins raised his eyebrows and puffed out his cheeks.

"Not that I could find out - I contacted them after he was dismissed and they told me that he hadn't even phoned them let alone sent in a letter of complaint."

"How many plants were missing, would you say?"

"About a thousand I would say; between seven hundred and fifty and a thousand - approximately thirty trays."

"How long had he been working here?"

"Nearly a year when he was sacked; we would have had three orders in that time, so he could have stolen thousands of plants during his time."

"That's a lot of plants - where would he have sold them?"

Jenkins spread his arms out wide.

"Car boot sales in Northamptonshire maybe, all cash no receipts, no questions asked." He tapped his nose.

"A long way from here then, so no chance of him being recognised."

"Presumably not."

"Clever I suppose; how much cash would he have received for the plants?"

"Around a pound a plant, I would have thought."

"Did you ever see him counting money or have wads of notes about his person?"

"No, never, he was quite tight-fisted with his cash."

"We'll have to check his bank accounts then to see whether there was ever a sudden influx of cash."

Knowles continued with the questioning as Barnes made a note about checking Pritchard's bank details.

"Jim, did Edward Pritchard have any girlfriends that he brought back to your place?"

"He had plenty of girlfriends, but he didn't bring them home."

"Where did he go with them then?"

"In the woods, in the monastery grounds, in Bunny Johnson's case in the greenhouse."

"She and Pritchard were lovers?" Barnes sounded shocked.

"I am sure they were; she enjoyed being taken from behind on the potting table, so I heard. She's called Bunny for a reason, Inspector." Jenkins smiled ruefully.

"And there was me imagining she enjoyed eating lettuce and carrots," smirked Knowles.

"You said in the monastery grounds - do you know where exactly?" asked Barnes.

"In the refectory."

"How do you know, did you follow them?"

"Pritchard and Gwendoline, yes, they were getting friendly on a blanket and I left them to it. I shouldn't have been there of course, but I know I wasn't the only one watching them as I saw someone with binoculars in the woods."

"This was when exactly?"

"In early Spring."

"Mother and daughter both being bonked by the same bloke - no wonder Sir Michael threw a wobbler and sacked him." Barnes shook his head.

"A lot of men would have done him harm," said Jenkins, "Sir Michael was the model of restraint."

"Perhaps he waited to get definite proof before doing him harm - setting up a meeting and then running him through with a sword."

"Why there though, why in the monastery?"

"Because that's where he corrupted Sir Michael's daughter?" suggested Knowles.

"I see."

"I am not sure I do, actually, I feel there's more to it than that - it's too easy. As you say, Sir Michael is a model of restraint, most of the time at least, and this murder has been planned for a few weeks, even months - this murderer is rather cold and calculating."

"How do you know it's been planned for months?" Jenkins sat forward - he was genuinely interested.

"The stolen sword, my friend, taken from the library, but never leaving the premises - I think the murderer planned this from the very day that Edward Pritchard was sacked."

"Which might mean that the sword could have some special significance for the murderer in relation to Pritchard," continued Barnes. "That's the line of investigation we should pursue."

"Thank you, Jim, for opening up this line of enquiry. That's all for the moment - can you please ask Gwendoline to join us?"

Jenkins looked pleased with himself as left the room holding his boots.

"How do you know the sword never left the property, sir?" enquired Barnes.

"I don't, Barnesy, but it's a big lump of metal to carry around and difficult to conceal about one's person, so I am just playing the percentages on this one. Jenkins is bound to tell everyone what we, sorry, I suspect and so the murderer is going to be anxious. Can you make a note to ask Dr. Crabtree if he found any soil in the wound?"

"OK, I won't ask why."

"It's just a hunch I have - I make no predictions about the outcome."

"What did you think about his plant selling story?"

"Yes, he seemed to know too much about it for it not to be foreign to him, so perhaps Jenkins took the plants himself, Pritchard found out and warned Sir Michael, who thought he was lying and trying to undermine his trust in his established gardener."

"Why would Pritchard do that, though?"

"Perhaps he fancied Jenkins' job and the house that came with it, so he would have something to offer Gwendoline?"

"Or someone else?"

"Maybe, but anyway, she's on her way I think."

Gwendoline smiled at the officers as she sat down. Her red hair tumbled over her shoulders and contrasted sharply with the light-blue pullover she was wearing. Her mascara had run slightly, but her eyes were clear.

"Gwendoline, in your statement you more or less

corroborate what Ellis said in his statement - how long was he out of the room for, would you say?"

"That's a difficult question to answer as I take an age to get ready for the shower - and then I washed for about ten minutes before cutting my toenails, but he was back in the room by then I am sure. You can tell when someone is in the room? You just know, don't you?"

"So it was about twenty minutes until you saw him again?"

"I don't think it was that long, perhaps fifteen minutes at the most, but I sensed he was in the room well before that."

"Funny things the senses sometimes," continued Knowles, "some are more reliable than others. Your room looks out towards the monastery, doesn't it? Did you see anyone out there at any time last night?"

"...Or hear any hooting?" added Barnes.

"Hooting - you mean owls, well as a matter-of-fact I did, just as I was opening the bathroom window before showering. There were church bells too; campanology classes by the sound of it."

"What time was this?"

"Around 11:15 to 11:20p.m."

"Did you see anyone in the grounds?"

"Well, the moon was out last night and it was clear with a few clouds around, and there was a slight breeze, so your eyes are bound to see tricks of the light."

"Does that mean you saw someone?" enquired Barnes.

"Well, perhaps, but it wasn't a definite sighting - I thought I saw a shadowy figure over by the north transept, but it was ephemeral."

"Does the monastery have a ghost?"

"It does, Sergeant, Brother Septimus who walks amongst the ruins at the full moon looking for his faith, they say, which he lost during the Dissolution of the Monasteries in the 1530s."

"A good ghost story always attracts a few extra visitors, doesn't it, Gwendoline?"

"This is true; I have seen him at dusk in the woods looking towards me."

"Really? He didn't have binoculars, did he?"

"I don't think Brother Septimus looks for his faith that closely, Sergeant."

"Right, just checking."

"Gwendoline," continued Knowles, "when was the last time you saw Edward Pritchard?"

"I haven't spoken to Edward for probably six months. The last time I saw him would have been three months ago when my father fired him at the weekend gathering we had then - the same people who are here now were here then."

"That's a coincidence, isn't it?"

"I don't think so, Inspector, it was arranged."

"Who would have 'arranged' it, Gwendoline?"

"Well, I am sure my mother had a lot to do with it, but Toby and Cedric would also have been in on the scheme as their same friends are here."

"What, all of them?"

"Yes, Inspector Knowles."

"Why have exactly the same people here - what's the reasoning?"

"You'd have to ask her."

"Was there a scene?"

"Edward was fired in a very humiliating way in front of a lot of people, so perhaps she thought that those people should have happier memories of a weekend here at Manton Rempville Hall. Hence, she invites them all back."

"And Edward Pritchard ends up dead at the start of the weekend," commented Barnes, looking suspicious.

"Could that have been planned, Gwendoline?" asked Knowles.

"Well, Inspector, there's a basic problem isn't there - the person who killed him must be local to steal the sword from the house, but then they wait until everyone is back again before committing the murder as though trying to indicate to us all that one of the out-of-towners is the killer."

"Isn't it more likely to have been the murderer inflicting the final humiliation on Edward by killing him when the same people who saw him so publicly sacked by your father are all back here again? Whoever did this really hated

Edward Pritchard and had a terrible sense of grievance against him."

Gwendoline reached into her handbag and took out a slightly damp handkerchief. She touched her eyes with the material before replying.

"I think you're right and I believe I know who did it, but I can't prove a thing of course."

"So, who do you think did it?"

"I am not saying without some kind of proof; I'd just sound like a village gossip and I despise those people."

"What's the basis for your theory?"

"Oh, it's just something someone said, which made me realise Edward was disliked more than I ever realised."

"So the person who killed Edward made a remark that you overheard?"

"No, someone said something about someone else and their attitude toward Edward."

"Wouldn't it be simpler to tell us your suspicions?"

"It's all hearsay - I will find out the reasons behind the remark and then let you know my suspicions - I am sure everyone else has their own ideas who did this terrible thing."

"Actually, you're the first to say anything about potential murderers."

Gwendoline nodded and a tear trickled down her cheek. She brushed her hair back and straightened her skirt.

"I was probably closer to him than anyone else, so I am feeling his loss more keenly than the others."

She dabbed her face with the handkerchief.

"I should probably go and get your next interviewee; who will it be?"

"If you could ask Miss Newton to come here that would be wonderful, Gwendoline."

She nodded and smiled wanly at the two officers as she left the room.

"Poor girl," said Knowles, "she obviously still had feelings for him."

"I wonder who she was referring to in her complicated remark about someone else gossiping about yet another person's attitude towards Pritchard?"

"I have no idea, Barnesy, that confused me no end, but I am concerned that she's going to find out more - that might put her in danger."

"Can we protect her, do you think?"

"That depends who the killer is - anyway, we shouldn't discuss this in case we are overheard, at least not here. She should be fine."

"What does Miss Newton say in her statement?"

"In her room in the coach house from 10:50p.m. onwards. The maid and the butler have rooms here in this building, while the others have estate properties in the village."

"I think I know where I'd prefer to be."

"Me too - well away from your employer. Anyway, here she is now, I believe."

Miss Newton stuck her head around the door jamb and smiled at the officers. She was in her mid-twenties and quite pretty even without any hint of make-up.

"Is this a good time, gentlemen?"

"There's no time like the present - what should we call you, Miss Newton? What's your name?" asked Knowles.

"Eleanor."

"Well, do sit down, Eleanor."

"Thank you, Inspector."

"Why do they call you Miss Newton then?" asked Barnes.

"Well, it's because the Johnsons are aware that in this age of equality they shouldn't just call me 'Newton' as it's demeaning, yet they are also aware that there should be some way of distinguishing between members of the family and staff, so they feel they can't call me 'Eleanor' either - hence 'Miss Newton' is the compromise."

"I wish I hadn't asked now, but thanks for explaining."

"Lady Johnson explained it to me a few days after I joined the staff."

"Last night you were in your room here at the coach house from 10:50p.m. onwards. Did you see anyone around outside?"

"I didn't see anyone around, though I heard a couple of cars arrive at different times..."

"Can you remember the time on each occasion?"

51

"The first was at 11:10p.m. and the other at 11:25p.m. - I have a bedside alarm, you see."

"Did you hear any church bells or hoots from owls?"

"Bells, yes - when I was walking over from the Hall at around 10:40p.m. they were pealing, I think is the term. As for hoots from owls, well, I heard some hoots, but I am not sure they were from owls as they sounded slightly too human."

"You mean the hoots were a signal or trying to get someone's attention?"

"Perhaps - they were quite close by on the monastery side of the Hall."

"Did you think to investigate?"

"Well, I did begin to walk around towards the lower study, but I thought I saw someone standing there and so I melted back into the shadows and came over to my room."

"Who was it?" Barnes leaned forwards in eager anticipation.

"I couldn't really see - their attention seemed to be on the upper floor."

"Which part of the upper floor?"

"The bedroom above the lower study, where Cedric and his friends are staying."

"Was there anyone up there?"

"I didn't stay to find out."

"Were you surprised that Edward Pritchard was murdered?"

Miss Newton crossed her arms.

"I was not - for a start he made up a nasty rumour about myself and Cedric being lovers that simply was not true…"

"And how do you know Pritchard started this story?" enquired Knowles.

"I saw Pritchard talking to Lady Johnson, who then glanced at me with a look of horror. Later Cedric told me his mum had asked him about Cedric and myself. Mr. Fairfax also dropped a heavy hint that 'relationships' between staff and family were frowned upon. Pritchard was the only one who could have started this rumour."

"Where did you see Pritchard and Lady Johnson?"

"They were at the entrance of the greenhouse. He was standing closer to her than he should have been."

"What else did Pritchard do that would have made someone want to kill him?"

"Stealing plants, corrupting Gwendoline, trying to blackmail Mrs. Swarbrick and Wilkinson regarding their relationship…"

"What relationship?" Knowles glanced at Barnes.

"Well Pritchard reckoned that those two were at it whenever they had the chance just because they lived next to each other in the village."

Miss Newton shook her head as she said the words.

"And he tried to blackmail them?"

"He did, but I'm not sure any money ever changed hands - I don't think there was any relationship between those two; it was another rumour."

"Why would he start so many rumours about people?"

"Because either Wilkinson or Mrs. Swarbrick had seen Pritchard up to something that could get him into trouble."

"Is there anyone here this weekend who doesn't have some strong feelings - either love or hatred - towards Pritchard?"

"I wouldn't have hurt him, Inspector, I abhor violence, but I have to admit I was angry when I heard what he had been saying about me behind my back."

"Enough anger to run him through with a sword, Eleanor?"

She shook her head vigorously.

"No, Inspector. Besides, where would I get a sword from?"

"The library or the upper library I should say, from where it disappeared about three months ago at the same time as the previous gathering of all these people here today."

"Where would you hide a sword for that length of time?"

"Good question, Eleanor, I can't begin to think where you would hide it."

"Would you take it home with you or leave it here?"

"That would depend on where you live."

"I suppose it would."

"You've not seen anyone acting suspiciously in terms of keeping people away from a certain part of the house?"

"Nothing stands out in my mind."

"Really?"

"The only thing I can think of is that Mr. Fairfax tries to keep everyone away from the secret passage, but then he's always done that - not just for the last three months."

"When you say keep people away, what do you mean?"

"Well, he doesn't like people to hover around where the switch is, especially if there are guests. Mr. Fairfax is worried in case someone finds out about the passage that he thinks shouldn't do."

"I see – well, it is a way into the house if the switch is in the unlocked position."

"Indeed, but the entrance at the other end is difficult to find."

"Sergeant Barnes and I will have to try and find it then and test your theory." Knowles smiled at Miss Newton.

"I can show you if you like." Miss Newton looked keen.

"That's extremely kind of you, but we're both fairly independent people and I am sure that we'd like to find it ourselves."

Barnes nodded in an exaggerated manner as if to enforce what Knowles had said.

"So," continued Knowles, "that's all for now. Could you please send in Cedric Johnson to speak with us. Thank you, Eleanor, you can go back to being Miss Newton again."

Miss Newton stood up smiling and walked out of the room. When she had been gone for a few seconds, Barnes looked at Knowles.

"Why was she so keen to show us the outside entrance to the passage?"

"I think she knows where the sword was kept and wants us to work it out rather than her telling us, but I am not sure why unless she fears she will be overheard."

"Perhaps she's very honest and wouldn't want to try and lie if anyone asked her if she'd told the police about the sword's hiding place."

"Which can only mean she's told someone else already

about her suspicions. It's not something that would crop up in a normal conversation, is it?"

"She's potentially in danger then, especially if the other person is the murderer."

"We should ask her who she's been talking to about the sword when we've finished these interviews."

"I will make a note of that."

"I think Cedric's statement more or less mirrors Timmy Beauregard's, which is no surprise I suppose. I hear him now."

After a few seconds Cedric Johnson sat down opposite the two officers and rubbed his hands together.

"You've found out lots of information, I hope - so do you know who did it yet?"

"We have a better idea, I think," said Knowles calmly.

"You'll probably find out by the end of these interviews that everyone here today would have had a motive to murder Pritchard."

"And what would your motive have been, Cedric?"

"Well, one of my best friends, James, is gay and fell for Pritchard, who rebuffed him, so I might want revenge for that. I might hate Pritchard because he was corrupting my sister, Gwendoline, and encouraging her to marry beneath her. He was having a weird effect on my mother who seemed to have a strange infatuation with this sub-gardener. There's three reasons."

"What's the significance of using the sword as opposed to a kitchen knife?"

"It's an indication that the upper-class family will always prevail over the lower-classes in any power struggle. We use superior weapons, not your common-or-garden knives or guns."

"And you have to make that point to the intended victim, even though they'd never know what had killed them, they'd never know what upper-class, superior weapon they were being murdered by? That seems like a waste - wouldn't you want to brandish the cavalry sword in front of the victim for a good few seconds, so that they would understand the significance of the weapon that was being used to kill them and, by that fact, comprehend the social implications of their murder?"

"You mean let Pritchard see the sword before killing him?"

"Indeed I do; that didn't happen of course - Pritchard was run through from behind when he was standing still, not running away. I doubt Pritchard saw his murderer as the sword would have been difficult to conceal. If you saw someone drawing a sword you'd either run away or face the person. You would not turn your back."

"Is that how it happened, Cedric?" asked Barnes.

"I wasn't there, Sergeant, so I can't answer that question, but I do know Pritchard got what he deserved for the three reasons I outlined earlier."

"Where do you think the sword was hidden, after it was 'stolen' from the library?"

"That's a very good question, because it was searched for high and low; all the books were removed from the upper library and nothing was found."

"When was it stolen exactly?"

"It was taken when the previous gathering of all the people who are currently here took place three months ago. My father checked the sword's whereabouts on Monday after everyone had left, and he found it missing. He had previously checked three days earlier and the sword was still there."

"Had the lock been forced?"

"No, the cabinet had been relocked without any apparent force involved."

"Do you think someone took it away from the Hall and then brought it back?"

"I think it was here all along."

"Why do you think that?"

"Too difficult to transport safely from the murderer's perspective. Where would they hide it - in their bags? And imagine all the questions there would be if it were found."

"So where would you hide it within the Hall?"

"I am not sure, Inspector, perhaps in the upper study. There are some secret panels where you could secrete certain items."

"How many secret panels are there?"

"There are five that I know of, which when you press on them in the top right-hand corner open up to reveal a secret compartment. They were a security measure in the times when a document falling in to the wrong hands could lead to a beheading."

"Did you search them all after the sword went missing?"

"I did, but not at the same time, as some are difficult to reach and need a ladder. I had the feeling I was being watched when I searched some of the panels, so perhaps the thief moved the sword when I was away."

"If the sword was hidden in the panels, then wouldn't it indicate the thieving was an inside job, by which I mean it was done by a member of the household, or staff, and not by one of the houseguests?"

"It would, unless the thief had an accomplice."

"By telling us about the secret panels do you hope to show us that you're neither the thief nor the murderer?"

"I was hoping to be helpful - why are you separating the thief and the murderer, surely they are the same person?"

"Well, they might not be the same person; there's the accomplice theory and there's also the possibility that the thief wasn't intending to murder Edward Pritchard but someone else. However, the actual murderer found out where the sword was and saw an opportunity to use the sword to kill Pritchard."

"What?" Cedric looked shocked.

"Yes, it's possible, everyone seems to have assumed that Pritchard's murder was pre-meditated and yet it might not have been; it could have been a spur of the moment decision."

"So, who was the thief planning to kill - presumably someone who was visiting this weekend?"

"Presumably, as I am sure, like you, that the sword was here all along."

"This is getting quite scary." Cedric stroked his chin.

"Can you think of any reason why one of the visitors this weekend would have upset someone here so much that they would wait three months to kill that visitor?" asked Knowles.

"But which visitors would you be referring to - would you include me for example? I live here, but am away for around six months of the year."

"The visitors would be James, Basil, Henrietta, Gertrude and George."

"Not Timmy then, because he was supposed to be coming last time, but didn't make it."

"That's correct."

"I suppose Gertrude and George should be included as they've not visited the Hall in those three months, but who would they have upset last time?"

"Henrietta and Basil too - they're just teenagers."

Barnes winced as he was reminded of Henrietta's young age.

"Which just leaves James who is twenty - who could he have upset?" wondered Barnes.

"Well, Barnesy, the answer to that question is Edward Pritchard, who found his attention and intentions disgusting, but then that would mean Pritchard stole the sword or had someone take the sword for him. Anyway, I think we have taken up enough of Cedric's time for the moment – Cedric, could you please ask Henrietta Fairfax to pay us a visit?"

"I will gladly do that, Inspector, and thank you for discussing the case so openly with me."

"It's a pleasure, Cedric; we were just throwing a few ideas around and I think we might have come up with a plausible explanation of what happened."

"Excellent - thanks, Inspector."

Cedric left, whistling a merry tune. Barnes waited for him to get out of earshot.

"The thief and the murderer two different people? When did you come up with that idea?"

"It just occurred to me whilst I was talking; we were assuming that one person has been the thief and the murderer and perhaps the thief and murderer were different people," replied Knowles.

"How could Pritchard have stolen the sword though?"

"Perhaps Gwendoline or Bunny helped him?"

"And what would Pritchard tell them he was going to do

with the sword - he couldn't really say that he was going to murder someone with it, could he? And yet, what else can you do with it?"

"Yes, the problems would start when Pritchard asked them to hide it somewhere where he could access it. They would then ask him why they were stealing the sword now, if they were only going to hide it somewhere else."

"Because Pritchard couldn't access the cabinet where the sword was housed."

"What could he have told them that he was going to be using the sword for? What plausible reason could there be? Could he use it for gardening or as part of a fancy dress outfit?"

"I think I have to scrap the idea about Pritchard stealing the sword, but I do think the thief and murderer are two different people."

At that moment the beautiful countenance of Henrietta Fawcett appeared in the doorway and asked whether she might sit down.

"By all means, Henrietta, be our guest."

"Thank you, Inspector Knowles. Now, what did you want to ask me?"

Henrietta made herself comfortable in the chair.

"Regarding your statement, you mention going for a walk with Toby after returning from the pub last night around 11:30p.m. Where did you go and did you hear any hooting or bell ringing?"

"Well, you know we walked for around thirty-five minutes out towards the monastery and back again. I did hear some hooting around the monastery and the woods, which is normal I believe..."

"And were the hoots made by owls?" interjected Barnes.

"The hoots were definitely owls, Sergeant, and not human beings communicating with each other." Henrietta giggled slightly.

"Thank you, please continue."

"There were no bells although I might have heard some pealing bells earlier in the evening, but definitely not at that time."

"Did you see any shadowy figures near the monastery during your walk?"

"Well, Toby said he did and when he pointed some shapes out they did seem to be humans, but when I looked back I couldn't see them again, you know, they'd gone and you begin to wonder whether you had just been seeing some trees and bushes in the breeze."

"I'll bet," said Barnes, "but why did you start to walk away from those shapes that you had been previously heading towards?"

"Well, because we didn't wish to go any further."

"And who decided that?"

"I think Toby did; he thought that we should head back."

"You were happy with that decision?"

"I was, actually, because I was quite cold, you know, I was finding the breeze rather bracing."

"I can imagine; you don't think that Edward Pritchard was one of the people you might have seen in the monastery?"

"I couldn't categorically state whether the figures were male or female, let alone whether they were certain individuals, Sergeant."

"That's fair enough, I suppose, given the time of night."

"Yes, although there was quite an amount of moonlight."

"And when you got back to the Hall did you see anyone else around?"

"No, we didn't - we came around the north side of the Hall and straight in through the coach house door."

"Did Toby show you the entrance to the secret passage in the monastery?"

"No, Inspector, not on this occasion, but I already knew where that entrance was because I was shown it three months ago, when we were here last time."

"Who showed you the entrance then?" asked Knowles.

"I think Mrs. Johnson did when she gave us the 'tour' of the monastery. She waved her hand at it and said something to the effect 'and of course that's the entrance to the secret passage', but we didn't have the chance to explore it."

"You didn't come back later and have a look or walk through the passage from the house side?"

"No, we rather got the impression that Fairfax was watching the inside entrance to the passage like a hawk. He always appeared whenever we went into the lounge."

"I am sure he was being attentive."

"He was, but there was more to it than that."

"In what way?"

"He seemed obsessed by not letting anyone near the entrance."

"Well, I think that's everything for now, Henrietta. Could I ask you to please send Fairfax to see us next?"

"I will do so, Inspector - see you later, Sergeant Barnes."

"Right you are," said Barnes, looking embarrassed.

Henrietta almost skipped out of the room.

"What's the matter Barnesy, are you ashamed of fancying a teenager?"

"She looks so much older." Barnes looked so wistful.

"Yes, at least twenty-one if a day - what do you think of her statement?"

"Well, I don't understand why Bunny Johnson would show everyone where the outside entrance to the passage was - that seems really strange."

"I wonder who else was there on that tour?"

"All the guests, I would imagine, but I will make a note to ask them all and check."

"It seems like the secret passage was not very secret after all; perhaps that's why Fairfax was always hovering around the lounge entrance, to make sure that no one was flicking the switch from the inside."

"Yes, the secret passage that everyone knows about."

"You don't think Bunny Johnson was trying to indicate to someone that this was a good way to get into the house?"

"You mean for a secret tryst? Well, that's something you could ask her, I suppose. Why would she indicate that to someone who was already staying at the house, unless it was for future reference?"

"I don't think I will ask her that right away, Sergeant - I wouldn't want to offend her before it's necessary."

"But why do it? Why tell everyone that the entrance is there when they don't really need to know? Unless she knew that one person there was going to be using the secret passage for some reason and would need to know where the passage would come out."

There was a slight cough. The officers looked up and saw Fairfax poised in the doorway.

Knowles beckoned Fairfax into the room and indicated the seat opposite.

"Mr. Fairfax, do sit down, what is your first name?"

"My first name is Christopher, but you can call me Fairfax."

He sat down in the chair rather stiffly and placed his hands on his knees.

"I'd prefer to call you Christopher, if that's alright, because I like to keep things on a first name basis."

Fairfax nodded his agreement.

"Christopher, you were attending Lady Johnson last night until 11:00p.m. in the lounge. What was she doing?"

"Her Ladyship was reading, writing a letter, and planning the entertainment for the guests this weekend."

"And she needed you to be there for what reason exactly?"

"I was there in case Lady Johnson needed a drink or more paper. She also sought my advice regarding the plans for the guests."

"And what happened after 11:00p.m.?"

"I retired to my room here in the coach house and fell asleep almost straightaway."

"It must be a long day for you."

"I am used to it, Inspector."

"The secret passage starts in the lounge, doesn't it?"

"It does, Inspector Knowles, but no one used it in either direction last night as I would have noticed it."

"So you were in the room that entire time?"

"I was, however I did go into the kitchen at one point for some tonic to accompany the gin, but I was out of the room for a minute or less."

"There's a door from the lounge into the kitchen?"

"No, it was blocked off, so one has to go via the playroom and the hallway and then back again."

"But Lady Johnson remained in the lounge when you were going for the tonic?"

"Presumably, I wasn't there of course. The only difference was that Lady Johnson had placed her cardigan over her shoulders whereas it had been lying over the chair when I had left the room."

"Was the fire getting low?"

"No. I had made up the fire only ten minutes beforehand."

"Interesting. When you went outside to come over here to the coach house, did you see anyone around?"

"No, Inspector, I presumed everyone was out or asleep."

"Did you hear any bells or owls hooting?"

Barnes looked at Knowles with obvious disgust - that was meant to be his question.

Fairfax thought for a few seconds before replying.

"I heard both throughout the evening from around 9:30p.m. onwards. The lounge is on the correct side of the house for hearing the owls in the monastery and for hearing the bells of St Anthony's clearly."

"When did the bells finish, can you remember?"

"I can't remember exactly, because I think they were practicing and so they would be silent for a few minutes and then start the pealing again."

"And the owls?" interjected Barnes, glancing at Knowles.

"Well, Sergeant, they aren't as regular as the bells; there was plenty of hooting around 10:00p.m. I seem to remember, but then there was a lull until 10:45 when there seemed to be another bout."

"So you looked at the clock?"

"I did, because Lady Johnson remarked on the owls and how active they were."

"Did she now?"

"Yes, Sergeant."

"And what did you say?"

"I had to agree with Lady Johnson."

"And was this before you left to get the tonic for the gin?"

"It was about fifteen minutes afterwards, approximately."

"When you were in the lounge, did you ever look out towards the monastery?"

63

"I probably didn't as the curtains were closed."

"When did the sword go missing?" asked Knowles, changing the subject quickly.

"It went missing three months ago, when the current guests were also present for the weekend."

"And you know that because…?"

"I know that because the sword was there on the Friday before they arrived and was no longer there on the Monday afternoon once everyone had departed."

"And you checked this both times?"

"Yes, because household security is my responsibility and I was horrified when I found that a theft had occurred." Fairfax leaned forwards as he spoke these words,

"You instigated a search?"

"Indeed I did, but we found nothing, so we reasoned that one of the guests must have taken the sword as a prank."

"Who reasoned that?"

"Sir Michael and Lady Johnson did and I agreed."

"They decided that together or was one more forceful than the other?"

"Well, I think Lady Johnson said something to the effect that 'boys will be boys' and they agreed that the sword would turn up again soon enough."

"Which it did, of course, buried in the back of Edward Pritchard."

"That was most unfortunate."

"Why unfortunate?"

"Well, if I had known that there was a murderer around the place then I would have called the police in to pursue the culprit more assiduously."

"We would have certainly done that," assured Knowles.

"Who was Lady Johnson referring to when she said 'boys will be boys'?" asked Barnes.

"I am not sure, Sergeant, but I would think Master Cedric and his friend James Beauregard."

"And how would they have smuggled the sword out?"

"I don't know - in a bag perhaps, we wouldn't have searched them, of course."

"Of course."

"Perhaps they just walked out with the sword when no one was looking and placed it in their vehicle?"

"They wouldn't have placed the sword in the secret passage for later collection from the outside?"

"I watch the doorway into the passage from the interior of the house very closely and no one went into that passage during that weekend."

"How do you know?"

"Because I taped the switch in place and that tape wasn't tampered with."

"Can you be sure that you placed the tape before the sword was taken?"

"I placed the tape on the Thursday before the guests even arrived, Inspector."

"And the sword was still there?"

"I can't categorically state that, no, because I didn't immediately check, but the sword was there on the Wednesday when I cleaned it."

"So you were the last person to see the sword other than the thief and the murderer."

"You made it sound like they are two different people, Inspector."

"I did, didn't I? Does that surprise you?" Knowles grinned.

"It does, yes, because I would have thought the purpose of stealing the sword would have been to kill someone." Fairfax folded his arms.

"I am sure it was, but I am not convinced that the thief and the murderer are the same person."

"You mean that the thief hid the sword somewhere, but someone else stole it to kill Edward Pritchard?"

"Or someone stole the sword and then told the murderer where it was," Knowles suggested.

"Either way, someone in the household is in extreme danger right now." Fairfax looked truly concerned.

"Yes, either the thief who was the accomplice or the originally intended murder victim of the thief. Depending on which of the scenarios you believe."

"What do you want me to do?" asked Fairfax, looking anxious.

"Keep your ears open and your eyes peeled. Are there any other lethal weapons in the house?"

"There are some daggers in the same locked cabinet as that sword used to be in and they are still there - at least, they were the last time I looked."

"OK, Christopher, please go and tell Lady Johnson to come here to see us and then get those daggers and bring them here for us to take away."

"I will do as you ask, Inspector."

"Thank you."

Fairfax arose and walked solemnly out of the room.

Knowles waited for a few seconds before speaking.

"I think he's quite concerned about what might happen, you know. I think he has his suspicions about who did what and when."

"He's in a difficult position, isn't he? He can't really voice any opinions, other than to give 'advice' on plans for entertaining the weekend guests."

"So what questions did you want to ask Lady Johnson?"

"Well, she has her alibi for most of the evening from Fairfax, so besides asking her why she's called Bunny, my question would be why she invited the same people again for a long weekend in the country."

"Yes, exactly the same people, three months later."

"What about you, sir, what would you like to ask her?"

"Why she showed the guests the exit of the secret passage."

"What will we do after the interviews have been completed?"

"We inspect the secret passage, contact Forensics regarding soil on the sword, speak to Erin Beardy, find out about those bells, and remove those weapons for safe keeping. We should check some of the alibis too."

"Plenty to be done, then."

"As ever, Sergeant."

"I think I hear Bunny Johnson, sir."

Bunny Johnson walked into the room and sat down in front of the officers without being asked. She looked a little pale and her eyes looked a little watery.

"Have you any ideas, Inspector Knowles and Sergeant Barnes, who killed Edward?"

"We are still conducting our enquiries, Lady Johnson, and we have yet to hear from all your guests. Certain facts have come to light, however, and we need to investigate other lines of enquiry."

"Thought so," said Bunny Johnson, "you are nowhere near finding out who did it."

"Can you help us then, Lady Johnson? Why did you show the guests the exit of the secret passage when everyone was previously here three months ago?"

"Because people find out anyway, so it's best to come clean about the secret passage and where it comes out in the monastery grounds. That way people aren't scuffling around in the bushes all weekend, looking entirely in the wrong place."

"Yes, it must be frustrating not to find the entrance of a secret passage," replied Knowles.

"While we are talking about guests, what was the reason for inviting exactly the same people to the house for another weekend so soon after the previous weekend?" asked Barnes.

"Three months is hardly 'soon', Sergeant Barnes, and the previous weekend was such a great success that it seemed obvious to invite everyone again. I would have done it sooner, but not everyone was available."

"Who wasn't available?"

"Well, everyone wasn't available at certain times; this was the first weekend when everyone was available."

"If this gathering hadn't happened, would Edward Pritchard still be alive?"

Lady Johnson bit her lip for a few seconds before answering:

"Yes, I believe he would have been, but it's too late now, isn't it? Too late for poor Edward."

"Have you any idea who may have killed Edward?"

"Plenty of ideas, Inspector, many ideas but I can't prove anything."

"Who do you suspect?" asked Knowles.

"I can't bandy names around without some kind of proof."

"You could let us know your thoughts. Off the record."

"Wouldn't that be doing your job for you?" Lady Johnson seemed suspicious.

"We would welcome any assistance you may be able to provide."

Barnes glanced at Knowles and could tell his unnatural diplomacy was being tested again.

"Well, Inspector, where do I start? James Beauregard, he's gay, he fell in love with Edward three months ago but Edward spurned his advances and called him something rather unfortunate. James was upset, so either he or his brother Timmy could have sought revenge on Edward. Ellis knows how Gwendoline felt about Edward and might have decided to confront Edward. Henrietta was all cow-eyed whenever Edward was around and yet Edward was not interested in her, so either she or her brother Basil could have decided to do away with him - if she can't have him then no one else can. Jenkins might have decided to murder Edward because he was after Jenkins' job. Miss Newton believed that Edward had started a rumour about herself and my son, so resented Edward for that. And I understand that Mrs. Swarbrick and Wilkinson both detested Edward because he thought they were having an affair and told a number of people."

"And what about the family?" Knowles asked.

"My family were not involved in this sordid murder."

"And what was your relationship with Edward Pritchard?"

"I let him get too close to me, Inspector, and that was a mistake."

"And members of your family wouldn't resent that?"

"They didn't know - I was discretion personified."

"But they would surely notice - you refer to Edward Pritchard as Edward and all the other members of staff by their surnames. That's a noticeable difference."

"I am sure that I don't do that around my family?" A slight look of doubt crossed her face as she said this.

"Only one slip would be enough to alert your family to how you felt."

"The members of my family are not killers, Inspector."

"Someone is a killer in this household and we have to find out quickly who it is."

"Yes, Inspector."

"Who do you think took the sword, Lady Johnson?" asked Barnes.

"Well, when it happened, I thought one of the boys had taken it as a prank, but I am not so sure now."

"And where would it have been hidden?"

"I thought they would have taken it back to Harrow or Oxford with them and were always intending to return it. But I am not convinced now; I have a feeling the sword never left the Hall."

"What makes you feel that?" queried Barnes.

"The sword was obviously taken for a reason and not as a prank; it was taken so it could be used to kill someone."

"Why use the sword when a kitchen knife could have been used or one of the daggers?"

"Yes, I have wondered that; it's almost as though the family honour was at stake and Edward had to be killed by a symbol of that honour. By a symbol of family tradition."

"But you have said that the family weren't involved."

"I know, so someone made the killing look as though it was connected to the family when it wasn't."

"You believe the thief and the murderer were the same person?" asked Knowles.

Lady Johnson raised her eyebrows slightly as though she believed this was not possible.

"I don't know - I suspect that it largely depends on where the sword was hidden. If it was kept here, then the sword could have been found by someone else and either re-hidden as it were or left where it was until the murderer needed it."

"Yes, finding where the sword was hidden is of the utmost importance."

"When did the sword go missing, Lady Johnson?" Knowles was using a more soothing tone of voice now.

"Well, according to Fairfax, it disappeared at some point over the weekend when all our guests were here the first time around..."

"Apart from Timmy Beauregard," interjected Barnes.

"Yes, that's correct, Sergeant Barnes, Timmy wasn't here - he was taken ill at the last moment and couldn't come."

"And so he can be eliminated from our enquiries," said Barnes.

"For the role of the thief, perhaps, but not for the murderer."

"Someone new to the Hall is hardly likely to come across a sword that someone else has hidden, are they?"

"Someone new to a place sees things as they are rather than how he remembers them or how he would like them to be."

"A fresh pair of eyes might see something for what it actually is?"

"It's entirely possible, Sergeant."

"You mean hiding something in plain sight?" asked Knowles.

"Yes, Inspector."

"Interesting," said Knowles, "well, I think we've kept you long enough, Lady Johnson, can you please ask James Beauregard in to see us?"

"I will do, Inspector, I think he's going to be hopping mad with you - he was expecting to go first."

"Was he now - are you saying he was angry?"

"Nearly angry, I would say." Bunny Johnson balled her fists when she said this.

"Well you can't always get what you want, can you?" said Knowles, trying to sound like Mick Jagger, an effect that was lost on Barnes.

"I will leave now," said Bunny Johnson, smiling at Knowles' impression.

"What was the strange voice for?" asked Barnes after Lady Johnson had left.

"It was an impression of a famous singer, Sergeant," said Knowles, "a singer you might not have heard of."

"John Lennon, you mean?"

Knowles smiled and ignored Barnes' comment.

"So Sergeant, what do you reckon about her comments?"

"She didn't mention Fairfax in her list of people who had

reasons to kill Edward Pritchard, did she? Or herself for that matter."

"She did not, but I would imagine she feels her faithful retainer wouldn't hurt anyone. And she would never implicate herself, would she?"

"Not if she has any sense."

"And that woman has sense, Sergeant, but again, I am sure she's not told us everything."

"But then again, who has?" asked Barnes.

"Well, here we are at last," said James Beauregard, sitting down with great impatience. "I distinctly remember asking to be interviewed first, not last."

"As it says in the King James Bible, so the last shall be first, and the first last: for many be called, but few chosen."

"Matthew 20:16 - very good, Inspector, I wasn't aware country policemen went about quoting the Bible, especially the New Testament."

"Well this trip has been an education for you already, hasn't it?"

"Indeed it has - so I presume you've already heard that I had a supreme crush on the unfortunate Edward Pritchard?"

"It was mentioned."

"Yes, it was terrible - love at first sight, I don't recommend it."

"Which wasn't reciprocated?"

"It was rebuffed quite bluntly."

"And how did that make you feel?"

"Quite upset as you can imagine, but not sufficiently angry to terminate the object of those affections."

"But you would say that, of course."

"Indeed I would."

"You have an alibi for most of last night, James, because you were out with Cedric and your brother, Timmy. Were the three of you together the whole evening?"

"Most of the time, but I am sure Cedric went off to chat up the barmaid at one of the pubs we went to, or probably at both actually. He may have been gone for about fifteen minutes or so on each occasion."

"And you know about the secret passage?"

"Yes, Bunny Johnson showed us the external entrance when we were here three months ago."

"Did that strike you as odd?"

"Showing us the exit? No, I don't think so - it's no longer a secret, is it? If she hadn't shown us, we'd have wanted to explore the passage and found out where the exit was - so it was probably a good move on her part."

Knowles looked slightly puzzled.

"Which perhaps tells you that she wasn't a hundred per cent confident that the entrance within the house was entirely secure or was being watched at all times."

James chuckled. "I suppose so, Inspector, after all Fairfax doesn't sleep in the lounge, does he? We could always sneak down the stairs when he's asleep and flick the switch and we would be in."

Barnes rubbed his goatee beard and asked, "Who would the 'we' be?"

"At that time it would have just been Cedric and me, as Timmy wasn't there."

"And what was the reason Timmy couldn't come last time?"

James looked puzzled: "Didn't you ask him yourself? Well, on the Friday we were due to come up here he came down with the flu - just overnight, no prior symptoms or anything - and he felt terrible and so stayed at home in London."

Knowles leaned on the table and looked at Barnes with a smile. The brothers had coordinated their stories well. He then looked back at James and asked,

"Did you steal the sword and take it back home with you?"

"I didn't steal the sword. Funnily enough, I was shown the weapon, by Toby I think it was, and quite admired it. What struck me was the size of the sword - it was a lot bigger than I thought it would be. I think the shock of being stabbed with it would have killed poor Edward."

Barnes shot an inquisitive look at Knowles before asking James,

"And when were you shown this sword?"

"Well, it must have been on the Saturday in the morning after breakfast and before we were shown around the monastery by Mrs. Johnson and before we went to Sir Michael's golf club."

"Did Toby mention who had keys to the cabinet?"

James leaned back and looked at the ceiling, racking his brain for an answer. He then looked triumphant. "He did mention it - I think there were three - Sir Michael has one, Fairfax has another, and then there's a third on that huge key ring in the kitchen. There must be a hundred keys on that thing. It's almost impossible to unlock anything because all the other keys get in the way."

"I'll bet they do," said Knowles with a knowing smile, "I won't ask how you found that out."

"Just experimentation," said James, throwing his hands in the air as though it were a trifling experience, "that's the only way to learn sometimes."

Knowles and Barnes both chuckled.

"Well, James," said Knowles, "I think that's everything. As you are last, you can go and tell everyone that the interviews are concluded and they can go about their business. We may well wish to speak to certain people again, but that is all for now. Thank you."

James smiled and said: "I apologise for my little tantrum at the beginning, I do hope you won't hold that against me."

Knowles straightened the statements on the table and looked at him:

"Don't worry, we won't hold anything against you, thank you, James."

James stood up and shook hands with both of them. He left and was replaced within ten seconds by Fairfax, who looked distinctly worried.

"Inspector, I have some disappointing news. I checked the daggers and there were only three of them - they're here in this case - but the fourth is missing. It was there when I cleaned them on Wednesday."

Knowles took the proffered case and told the butler quite forcibly,

"Christopher, under no circumstances do you tell anyone what you have told me, just tell anyone who asks that the police have taken all the daggers for safe keeping and will return them when the murderer is apprehended. And by everyone I mean your employer and the other staff - just keep this information to yourself - no exceptions."

"I will, Inspector Knowles," replied Fairfax deferentially. "I will leave you to your deliberations." And with this he left the room.

"Right, Barnesy, when we get these daggers back to the station we should put a mark on each of them, just for our own protection in case the other dagger makes an appearance in someone's back."

Barnes nodded his agreement.

"So what do you reckon, sir?"

"I believe that our thief and our murderer are different people and that the thief was intending to kill someone, but his weapon of choice was taken on the spur of the moment by someone else and used for the same purpose as the thief was intending it to be used. I believe a number of people are in danger and we are going to have to act fast before someone else is murdered."

Chapter 3

Knowles placed the statements in a folder and asked Barnes to initiate the investigation of Edward Pritchard's bank accounts to see whether there were sudden influxes of cash. While Barnes was on the phone, Knowles phoned WPC Smythe to find out what she had discovered from Wilkinson's wife.

"Hello, Linda, did you speak to her? Right... Oh, so he did go out... at 10:40-ish for around fifteen minutes. Does she know where he went?... To Sir Michael's agent's house?... Delivering an item for the Hall? Well, that little titbit of information certainly slipped his mind. Thanks, Linda, can you come over here now? Yes, we'll be in the Hall looking at the secret passage. It's not that secret actually, everyone seems to know where it is. Oh, and can you bring a bottle of water and some snacks, we haven't been offered a single drink by the owners. Thank you. And one final thing, on your way here can you pop into the Red Lion and ask Syd Watt what time Jim Jenkins was in his pub last night?"

Knowles put the phone in his pocket and looked over at Barnes, who was concluding his conversation regarding Pritchard's accounts. Knowles looked out of the window and saw the spire of St Anthony's church through the trees; he made a mental note to find out when they'd been practicing last night.

"So that's the account search set up, sir," said Barnes. "It shouldn't take long for the records to come through."

"Right, thanks, Barnesy. It seems like our friend Wilkinson omitted to mention that he left his house for fifteen minutes or so last night to visit Sir Michael at his agent's house."

"And Sir Michael omitted to mention it too."

"Indeed, so I think I will send WPC Smythe around to see the agent just to corroborate what actually happened last night."

"Sounds like a plan, sir. Should we go and inspect that secret passage now?"

"Yes, from both ends as it were, and we should ask Miss Newton to accompany us on the external excursion and ask her to whom she has been voicing her concerns."

After stopping to place the daggers in the sports car, Knowles and Barnes walked over to the Hall, walked through the play room into the lounge and found Fairfax waiting for them.

"You were expecting us, Christopher?" asked Knowles.

"I thought I heard you say you would want to inspect the secret passage, so I thought I would show you myself," said Fairfax.

"You seem like the best person for the job," said Knowles, "but before you show us can you ask Miss Newton to make herself available so she can show us the external exit?"

Fairfax opened his mouth as if to object, but thought better of it and instead said, "I will let her know." He disappeared from the lounge and came back a minute later.

"I have asked her to be ready in fifteen minutes. Inspecting the passage won't take long."

Fairfax picked up the torch he'd placed on the desk previously.

"Gentlemen, the switch for the passage is here."

Knowles and Barnes looked at the wall lamp Fairfax indicated. The butler lifted the plaque the lamp was attached to and swung it to the left. This action revealed a small lever that Fairfax pulled down gently with no discernible effect.

The butler restored the plaque to its original position and headed over to the bookcase by the window. He placed his hands under the shelf containing the third row of books and lifted it slightly. This section of the bookcase moved backwards and then slid to the right revealing a set of stone steps. Barnes looked genuinely excited and Knowles decided to let him follow Fairfax. Once the three men were inside Fairfax moved the shelves back again so that a casual observer in the lounge wouldn't notice anything amiss.

The steps went straight down for about twelve feet and then took a ninety degree turn to the left. The secret passage stood before them heading straight towards the monastery. It was about six feet high and wide enough for just one person to pass along it at once. Most of the interior was covered in bricks. The three men started to walk along the tunnel.

"Would these bricks have always been here?" asked Knowles.

"The original tunnel was just dug out of the earth with occasional stone arches for support, but parts collapsed and had to be strengthened with bricks," replied Fairfax.

"Is the whole tunnel covered in bricks then?" said Barnes, taking care not to hit his head on the ceiling.

"Most of it is near the house, but at the other end it's almost all original."

Five minutes later the three men arrived at the monastery end and saw a wooden ladder propped against the wall. Fairfax climbed up and lifted a wooden covering, allowing the officers to see the light grey sky and some of the taller trees around the monastery. Knowles quickly looked around at the walls and prodded the earth with his finger. The dirt was hard, but a sharp implement would certainly penetrate it and be held in place.

"I think we should get the uniforms with some lights in here to see if they can find a hole in the tunnel wall where the sword could have been hidden," commented Knowles. "I would really like to find out whether this was the place."

"Wouldn't the handle have stuck out?" asked Barnes.

"Maybe it could have been hidden by some of the bricks in an arch?" wondered Knowles, "especially close to the ground as the torch doesn't throw its light down to the ground, if you notice."

"There's always that possibility, sir," said Barnes. "I'll phone them and ask them to come over here this afternoon."

"Will you get reception down here?" asked Fairfax.

"I'll try," said Barnes, "you never know. It depends on how far under the surface we are."

"Can you open the exit door again, please, Christopher?" asked Knowles.

Fairfax lifted the door and Barnes walked around for a few seconds.

"There's a signal under the door, but it goes within two strides down the passage," reported Barnes. "I'll test it again periodically on the way back."

"Right, thanks, Christopher, let's head back and see if WPC Smythe has arrived."

Fairfax handed the torch to Knowles and the three men headed back to the Hall. Knowles played the torch around some of the thinner arches and saw that most of them were two or more bricks thick for additional strength.

"Any signals, Barnesy?" asked Knowles.

"Occasionally, there's a weak signal under those thinner arches, but not enough to make a phone call or to access the Internet," replied Barnes.

========

Knowles climbed up the steps back into the lounge and switched off the torch. Miss Newton and WPC Smythe were looking out of the window towards the monastery. WPC Smythe's police cap made her look a little incongruous in the surroundings. She didn't like wearing the cap as it masked the fact that she'd recently coloured her hair auburn.

"Hello, Eleanor, are you ready for our little excursion to the monastery?" asked Knowles.

"Definitely, it's a lovely stroll; I was just showing Linda the way we will be going."

"Unfortunately, Linda has a little excursion of her own to go on - are you OK, Linda, you look a little cold, have you just arrived?"

"I have been here about ten minutes. I was cold about five minutes ago, but I have warmed up again, sir."

"Right, I would like you to go over to Stoney Stafford and speak to Sir Michael's agent. Where does he live, Christopher?"

"He lives on London Road, number 1 London Road; the house is called Rose Cottage. It actually backs on to the woods that you would reach if you head over to the monastery and then turn due north. It's a ten minute walk at the most. You just have to be careful when you cross the road."

"Well, I will be driving, so I am sure I will find it. What did you want me to ask him, Inspector?"

"Let's discuss that as we leave. Barnesy, Eleanor, are you ready?"

"Did you need me for anything further, Inspector?" asked Fairfax.

"Not at the moment, Christopher, thank you for your help."

When everyone reached Barnes' car, Knowles turned to Miss Newton and asked her to wait for them on the eastern side of the Hall. When she was out of earshot, Knowles gave his orders.

"Barnesy, give WPC Smythe those daggers now."

Barnes unlocked the boot and gave the daggers to Smythe, who placed them in her vehicle.

"Linda, when you have finished with the agent go back to the station and give these weapons to the staff sergeant, who should place them under lock and key. Make sure he places an identifying mark on those daggers before making them secure. Barnesy, ask uniforms to get over here and tell them to bring some arc lights, a generator, and their own torches. Tell them to go to the monastery car park and wait for instructions."

Barnes nodded and phoned straightaway. Knowles turned back to Smythe.

"What did Syd Watt at the Red Lion say about Jim Jenkins?"

"He just said Jenkins was in the pub last night around 10:15 for about half-an-hour or so and that he had a couple of pints of best bitter."

"Sounds about right, Linda, anyway at the agent's just ask him what happened last night, what he and Sir Michael did, and whether anyone else visited them at any time. If someone else interrupted them, please try and find out the exact time it happened. Oh, and before you go, do you have the water and snacks I asked for?"

Linda Smythe smiled and thought that six months ago Colin Knowles would have asked for the food first and then munched away while giving her instructions.

"When you interview the agent," added Knowles, "I'd take off your cap so you look less official and more feminine - he might warm to you more that way."

Knowles gladly accepted the proffered water and biscuits from Smythe. He shared them with Barnes when he'd finished his call to the uniform branch.

"Here you are, Sergeant Barnes, some Jaffa cakes to keep you going until we go to the pub later."

"Thanks, sir, I am more interested in the water; they couldn't even offer us a cup of tea in there, could they?"

"No, they don't exactly make you feel wanted, do they? Oh, here's Eleanor waiting for us. Tell you what, you start off with her and I'll just call Dr. Crabtree regarding soil in the wound."

Barnes walked over to Miss Newton and they soon headed off towards the monastery.

Knowles rang Dr. Crabtree:

"Hello, Kevin, it's Colin - I am fine and yourself?... Oh good, glad to hear it. Well, why I rang - that sword and the wound, did you find any soil or dirt either on the sword or in the wound? On the sword, the soil might have been around the hilt and not on the blade necessarily... Right, well if you could check again that would be wonderful. Thanks, Kevin, yes, do call me when you find out. Thank you."

Knowles started to walk over to the monastery and caught up with Miss Newton and Barnes after about a minute. Knowles listened in for a few seconds as she was talking and then asked a question.

"Eleanor, I know you may have told Sergeant Barnes already, but where exactly are we heading?"

"We are heading towards that group of seven mature trees; the exit is under the branches of the third one on the left." Eleanor pointed in a north-easterly direction.

"Right, thank you, Eleanor. So who have you been talking to about the possible location of the sword after it was stolen?"

Miss Newton went quite white and almost stopped walking:

"I didn't say that in my interview, did I, Inspector?"

"No, not in so many words, but why were you so keen to show us the external exit of the secret passage?"

"Well, I thought you should know where it was; it's about three minutes to the refectory from the exit." Miss Newton tried to be convincing but failed.

"Do you think that the sword was hidden in the secret passage, Miss Newton?"

Miss Newton took out her handkerchief and dabbed away a few gentle tears.

"It has to have been, doesn't it? You couldn't walk around with a sword in your hand in case someone saw you; you couldn't hide it about your person. It had to have been left in the passage for future use."

"You believe it was taken from the library, sorry, the upper library, and moved to the passage, where it lay for three months waiting for the thief to become a murderer?" asked Knowles.

"I don't believe so. I think it was hidden somewhere in the Hall and then moved last night to the passage." Miss Newton looked around as though she was worried about being overheard.

"Who by?" asked Barnes.

"I am not sure, Sergeant Barnes, I thought that someone went into the lounge last night around 6:00p.m. and they never came back out again. After about twenty minutes I went in there and nobody was about. I know because I was arranging the flowers in the hallway outside the door into the play room, which is the only way out of the lounge."

"Do you know where the person came from?"

"I don't know for sure. I had dropped a couple of cut flowers on the ground and was kneeling down to recover them when the person went in there. They must have thought the coast was clear."

"The timing is immaculate; they must have been watching you," said Barnes. "Where exactly were you kneeling down?"

"I was on the lower library side of the hallway, kneeling behind the table - I couldn't see through to the play room side as the legs are too thick."

"Did you hear anything?"

"I had my earbuds in, Inspector, listening to my i-Pod, so no, I didn't hear anything. And I didn't think anything of it either as I expected the person to come out again and I couldn't have missed them because I was standing up the rest of the time looking right at the door where they would have come out."

"Who was the next person you saw?"

"It was the three boys who came down the stairs from their bedroom, just after I came out of the lounge. Then Toby and his friends and Sir Michael's parents were in the hallway and Fairfax and Mrs. Swarbrick were in the kitchen."

"Why did you go in there?" asked Knowles.

"Someone asked for some tonic for the gin…"

"Which was in the lounge," finished Barnes.

"Yes, it would have been - oh, you mean someone was in the lounge and could have flicked the switch back again before Fairfax spotted something?"

"Yes, they needed to distract whoever else was in there and so the tonic would have been one way of doing it," said Knowles.

"Who asked for the tonic, Eleanor, can you remember?"

"I can't, Sergeant Barnes, but I will let you know when I do."

Barnes looked at Knowles with alarm.

By now the three of them had arrived at the group of seven trees. Miss Newton showed the two officers where the exit door was hidden under some leaves. Barnes lifted up the door and wondered whether there might be some incriminating fingerprints on it. Knowles obtained a branch from the ground and propped open the door so that the uniformed investigation team would know where the passage was located.

"Do you have the feeling we're being watched?" asked Knowles.

"Why would anyone do that?" asked Miss Newton.

"That depends on who it is," said Barnes, "did someone follow us or is it someone watching through binoculars, sir?"

"Binoculars, Sergeant, from the woods over there. I thought I saw the light reflect from the lenses - don't look as that will give it away."

Barnes was about to turn around, but stopped himself just in time. He pretended to be looking into the open door of the secret passage.

"Is Linda able to help? She's heading over to the agent's place, isn't she?" he asked.

"She's probably there by now - I will look around the general vicinity again," replied Knowles, "and see if they are still there."

Knowles casually looked around the monastery, scanning the horizon like a lookout on an ocean-going ship.

"They've gone, I think - can you see anyone in the woods, Sergeant, anyone walking back to the Hall?"

"The woods are quite dense there, Inspector, so it's very difficult to see anything," commented Miss Newton. "I think it was probably Timmy Beauregard; he's very interested in bird-watching."

"Who else owns a pair of binoculars in the Hall?" asked Barnes.

"There's about six pairs in the sports room that people use when they go to the races," replied Miss Newton.

"All the same manufacturer?" queried Knowles.

"They all look the same to me," said Miss Newton, "but I am not sure if they are all the same manufacturer."

Barnes' phone rang and he walked away a little to take the call.

"How are you feeling, Eleanor?" asked Knowles, "are you worried about your own safety?"

"I am worried, Inspector - I have a feeling the person who asked for the tonic might be the murderer."

"Well, the way you described what happened with people arriving, I think it's fair to say that the person who asked for the tonic is not the murderer, but that the person they were with is the murderer or is quite likely the murderer. The murderer would have asked the other person to obtain some tonic, so they could be alone in the lounge for a few seconds to flick the switch and replace the tape before Fairfax noticed. I think you're going to be fine."

Barnes walked back to Knowles and Miss Newton.

"Uniforms are almost here, sir, so shall we help them set up?"

"Yes, Sergeant, let's do that. Miss Newton, thank you for accompanying us on the walk. We will help our uniformed section set up some lights so they can search the monastery end of the passage for possible hiding places for the sword."

"Right, well, I will go back to the Hall - and if I think of the person who asked for the tonic I will let you know straightaway."

As Miss Newton headed back to work, Knowles and Barnes walked across the monastery grounds to meet their colleagues from Scoresby police station in the car park.

========

As Knowles and Barnes were walking to the car park, not one mile away WPC Linda Smythe was knocking on the front door of Sir Michael Johnson's constituency agent, Gerald Heath. He lived in an 18th-century house made from traditional Cotswold stone. The house was in about two acres of grounds and Smythe could see the mixed deciduous trees that headed towards Manton Rempville Hall and the monastery.

After about thirty seconds Gerald Heath himself came to the door and stared through the spy hole - WPC Smythe showed her identification to the door and felt silly when she did it. The shadow behind the door moved slightly and Smythe heard bolts moving and then the door was opened slowly by Mr. Heath. He was a man roughly sixty years old wearing pinstriped trousers and a green cardigan over a crisp, white shirt.

"Yes, officer, how can I help you?"

"You are Sir Michael Johnson's agent, Mr. Heath?" Smythe smelled cigar smoke wafting through the doorway and couldn't help noticing that the man's moustache was the colour of old tobacco. This contrasted with his general pale demeanour.

"I am, constable, is he in trouble or something?"

"No, Mr. Heath, I would just like to verify he was with you last night."

"Oh, I can provide Michael with his alibi for the murder last night. Yes, he was with me most of the evening, until 11:15p.m."

"You know about the murder then?"

"Yes, Michael phoned me about it - shocking thing to happen in a tight-knit community such as ours, but Edward Pritchard did make many enemies during his short stay at the Hall, so I am not completely surprised."

"You were in Sir Michael's company for the whole evening?"

"Absolutely, I think we even went to the toilet at the same time as we were leaving the restaurant." Mr. Heath rubbed his grey hair as if slightly discomforted about revealing this fact to the police.

"That's amazing, isn't it?"

"It is." Mr. Heath smiled. Smythe looked at his teeth and reminded herself never to start smoking.

"Did anyone come here last night for Sir Michael?"

"Someone came to the door around 10:30 and Michael said it was for him, so he answered it himself."

"Who was it?"

"Michael never did say; I am not sure how the person knew to come here as Michael didn't use his phone for the whole evening. In fact, now I think about I'm not sure how Michael himself knew, unless it was all pre-arranged, of course."

"Was it his chauffeur - did a car drive up to the house?"

"I didn't hear anything at all - it could have been anyone. They could have parked on the street and just come down the path to the door."

"I suppose so - it's a bit unusual not to tell your host who the visitor is, though."

"Michael is a very private person."

"Was Sir Michael carrying something when he came back to you, was something delivered?"

"I don't believe he was carrying anything when he returned, so I would presume not unless he took it straight to his car. He was only absent from the room for two minutes."

"Well, thank you, Mr. Heath. I hope I haven't taken up too much of your time."

"Not at all, I am always happy to help the police with their enquiries." Mr. Heath managed to make this statement sound genuine as he closed the door.

WPC Smythe inhaled fresh air for the first time in two minutes - she couldn't believe Mr. Heath hadn't even come close to inviting her inside. She went back to her car and wrote down the salient points of her conversation before heading off to Scoresby station to put the daggers under lock and key.

=========

Back at the monastery the police had managed to move a portable generator to the entrance of the secret passage. This powered four strong lights that illuminated the first fifty yards of the passage.

"What are we looking for exactly, Inspector?" asked Sergeant Roberts, who was in charge of the search team.

"Well, Sarge, it's either a place where you could conceal a three foot long sword in its entirety or a hole in the dirt made by the sword. Bear in mind that this hole would be in a place where the handle wouldn't be seen by anyone passing by."

"This passage was well used then?"

"We have to assume so."

"Right, this shouldn't take too long then as I don't see many hiding places."

"There are more than you realise, Sarge, because some of the arches have gaps between them where a sword could have been hidden."

"How big will this hole be?"

"About two inches high and around a quarter of an inch wide, perhaps - it might be slightly wider than that if the person who took the sword had to waggle it around before removing it."

"Right, well let's see what we can find for you, Inspector. Come on lads, let's all take a ten yard stretch of the tunnel."

The five searchers headed down the ladder clutching their individual lights and disappeared from view.

"I hope they find something," said Knowles, "or otherwise I am going to look rather idiotic."

Barnes smiled and looked across to the refectory, where Edward Pritchard had been killed.

"I'm sure they will. These trees provide plenty of cover for the murderer; you can see the refectory from here. You could then use the walls as cover and arrive at the refectory without being seen."

"And then where do you go afterwards? Across to the car park and through the woods to the north of the Hall?"

"I suppose so, sir, but you would have to be really careful as there were people arriving back all the time."

"Indeed you would, but we are assuming, are we not, that the murderer went back to the Hall rather than heading into the village?"

"Yes, we are assuming that, sir, but doesn't it have to be someone from the Hall, given that Eleanor was asked to get more tonic by one of the people staying there? Jenkins or Wilkinson wouldn't ask one of the family or one of the guests for more tonic, now would they?"

"That is true, Barnesy, but Jenkins or Wilkinson or indeed someone else entirely could have seen the thief coming out of the passage and heading back to the Hall, found the sword in the passage, and then used it instead of the thief."

"With respect, sir, that's not likely as Jenkins or Wilkinson wouldn't know there was a sword down there."

"Well, unless they saw the thief with the sword heading into the Hall and then saw them afterwards without it?"

"So that would mean the sword was hidden outside somewhere or in the coach house?"

"That's a bit flimsy, isn't it - no, you are correct Sergeant, the person who went down the passage, hid the sword, and then went back into the Hall from the outside must have been intending to murder Pritchard and must be a member of the internal staff, the family or a guest. Jenkins and Wilkinson are off the hook."

"And Miss Newton - couldn't she be making up all the tonic business, just to throw us of the scent?"

"Again that's possible, but I don't think she's lying. I think she's quite fearful about being the next victim."

"So that's three people we can eliminate - what about Mrs. Swarbrick? She wouldn't be ordering people around in the lounge, would she?"

"Probably not, no, so that's four people. I think that's about all we can do for now, Sergeant."

"We can't eliminate Fairfax, can we?"

"I don't think we can; he might politely ask someone and they would happily oblige."

"I think you're right."

"The next item to consider, Barnesy, is that the person who stole the sword must have arranged to meet Edward Pritchard there."

"Yes, so the murderer must have been able to contact Pritchard and meant enough to Pritchard for Pritchard to arrange a meeting with them."

"Is it possible that the murderer found out that Pritchard was meeting someone else and got there first?"

"In that case, sir, wouldn't the person who'd arranged the meeting have found Pritchard dead?"

"Not if they saw the murderer heading to the monastery with the sword. They'd have guessed what was happening and gone back to the Hall."

The wind blew through the trees and both men shivered. The sun was beginning to set on this late autumn day.

Sergeant Roberts poked his head out of the open entrance and shouted to Knowles and Barnes.

"Inspector, I think we have found your hiding place."

Knowles and Barnes walked over to Sergeant Roberts and followed him down the ladder into the passage.

"Young Edwards found the place; it's in the third archway high up - one of the bricks has been hollowed out by the looks of it. This would likely hold the handle; there's also a hole in the soil much as you described it. I will show you."

Knowles and Barnes followed Sergeant Roberts down the passage to a brightly illuminated arch, which comprised two rows of bricks set six inches apart. One of the bricks in the row nearer the house had indeed been hollowed out to hold the handle of the sword.

"What a hiding place - you would have to be walking towards the house to even stand a chance of seeing the handle."

"I think the handle might have been wrapped in a red cloth, as there's a couple of threads attached to the brickwork," said Roberts.

"Sounds about right from what I remember Dr. Crabtree saying; isn't that right, Barnesy?"

"It is, sir - I see that there is a hole in the dirt where the actual blade would have gone."

"Right, so now we know some of what happened - the murderer came along the passage, placed the sword in the hiding place, and then went out of the exit and headed back to the house. Later, they walked back over here - not coming along the passage – but found they'd been beaten to it," said Knowles.

"And they did that because they knew they were going to be out that evening and couldn't rely on the lounge being empty when they returned," concluded Barnes.

"Sounds like you have how it was done and all you need to do now is work out why and who," mused Roberts.

"I think the when it was done is the next thing to work out; I think almost everyone was out and about last night at some point without an alibi. If we can work out when it was done then that will eliminate some people and not others," said Knowles.

"We should try to match the bells that people heard with the time they said they heard them and see if anything matches," replied Barnes.

"Yes, we will do that. Anyway, Sarge, I think your work here is done, so thanks for your time. We'll help you carry the equipment back to the vans and then head over to the Hall and pick up our vehicle. We should head over to St Anthony's and see if anyone is around."

"Thank you, Inspector; we appreciate your appreciation, if you like."

"That's OK, Sarge; we're all in this together after all."

Knowles and Barnes helped carry the generator back to the police van and waved goodbye to their uniformed colleagues, before heading through the woods to the Hall. Knowles suddenly stopped.

"This is more or less where the person with the binoculars was standing, Barnesy. Can you see any footprints?"

"Not clearly, no, but there is a bubble gum wrapper here which looks fairly fresh to me and is lying on top of the grass, which indicates it's been dropped here today, in fact fairly recently."

"Right, well I have only seen one person chewing any kind of gum around here, so I shall have to talk to him about his recent activities."

Before Barnes could ask whom he meant, Knowles' phone rang. It was WPC Smythe.

"'Allo, Linda, you saw the agent... He left you on the step and blew cigar smoke over you, charming... Did he now?... But he didn't see Wilkinson... Right, thanks, Linda, see you later."

"What was that about cigar smoke?" enquired Barnes.

"The Conservative agent kept Linda on the step throughout their entire conversation and blew cigar smoke over her. However, she was able to discern that last night Sir Michael was expecting a guest, who duly arrived, and Sir Michael kept their identity hidden from his agent. In other words, Sergeant Barnes, Wilkinson does not have an alibi for last night. Not yet, at least, until we ask Sir Michael, of course."

"Strange Sir Michael wouldn't tell his agent, a trusted advisor, who was at the door of the agent's own house."

"Yes, but the rich are different from we peasants, Barnesy."

"Yes, sir, they have more money and more time on their hands."

"And more skeletons in their cupboards."

"And more secrets in their passages."

"My, you are on form today, Sergeant Barnes."

"Thank you, sir; your views are rubbing off on me."

"I'm glad something is, anyway, enough of the banter, do you think the bubble gum wrapper was a plant for us to find?"

"No, because the only person who would do that would be the murderer. They would be trying to implicate the gum-chewer as the person who was watching us rather than the murderer."

"You are probably right, but it just seems too obvious to me - a wrapper lying on the grass like that; surely the person who dropped it would have noticed?"

"Not everyone is as aware of their surroundings as you are, sir."

"Thank you, Sergeant, but I would have thought that the purple would stand out against the green grass sufficiently for anyone to notice."

"And just who was chewing gum, I can't remember seeing anyone?"

"Well, I did, when we first went into the lower library, one person was chewing for a few seconds only."

"You're not going to tell me, are you?"

"Not at the moment, Barnesy. Just try remembering what you saw when you went into that room - everyone was looking at us."

"They certainly were. Oh, almost tripped up there... this grass is certainly uneven. If the murderer came back this way, wouldn't they have very muddy or wet footwear when they got back to the Hall?"

Knowles wrapped his coat tightly around him as the wind got up.

"Yes, they would, and they'd be extremely cold too and wouldn't warm up very quickly. You would expect their partner or roommate to notice this, of course."

"Unless they were in the shower and then their partner had a shower immediately afterwards to warm up."

"Yes, that would be one way of doing it - another way would be to get into bed fully clothed and pretend to be asleep."

Barnes suddenly stood still and looked back at the monastery,

"Did you hear a hoot, sir, an owl's hoot?"

"I did, Sergeant, a real one too, not a human imitation. I wonder where they're nesting."

"Will we see them flying around?"

"Not if they have anything to do with it."

"I wonder if they have been disturbed by someone?"

"Probably by the uniforms driving off."

"The hoots that were heard last night, were those real, do you think?"

"Most of them, but not all I am sure. I think there was an arranged signal between the murderer and Pritchard, which was probably a hoot."

"You think that Pritchard willingly met the murderer?"

"I don't, Barnesy, I think he was expecting someone else. We should have a look at his place tomorrow and see if there are any emails from his admirers. Anyway, I am putting my hat on, it's freezing." Knowles placed his dark red bobble hat over his hair in a slightly self-conscious manner as they were now close to the Hall and in sight of anyone looking out of a window.

"Sir, it's taken us seven minutes to get back, so I reckon it would be a round-trip of about seventeen minutes for the murderer as they would have to pick up the sword from the passage and then sneak up on Pritchard in the refectory."

"That's a fair while for someone to be away from the person or persons they were with. The combination of being cold, having wet shoes, and being away for around seventeen minutes narrows down the number of suspects even more. Who would be able to get away with this? Sir Michael Johnson, Bunny Johnson, Ellis Hardaker perhaps, Basil Fawcett, and that's it. Basil doesn't have an alibi for the whole time Toby and Henrietta were on their walk - Ellis could have done it if he'd changed his footwear in his car afterwards, Sir Michael was on his way back from his agents, and Lady Bunny was on her own after Fairfax left her for the evening."

"Should we search Ellis Hardaker's car and Basil Fawcett's room for wet footwear, sir?"

"We could, but does that prove they were the murderer - they would just say they were walking in the monastery grounds, minding their own business, and their shoes became wet in the long grass."

"And when would Basil Fawcett have done that, given he was out last night with his friends?"

"This morning before we arrived or last night after he arrived, but before he went out with his friends - perhaps he decided to reacquaint himself with the grounds."

Knowles and Barnes were outside the lower study and were able to verify that there were no statues outside on the patio, but there were a number of muddy footprints heading in various directions, which didn't help their investigations. The wind swirled the remaining leaves around their feet. A couple of ravens cawed in the nearby trees.

"So Miss Newton stood here and saw a figure looking up at the upper study at around 10:40 - I wonder who that could have been?" wondered Barnes.

"You don't think it might have been Edward Pritchard hoping that Gwendoline was in the bedroom next door?"

"How would he have known she was there?"

"He wouldn't have known - perhaps he thought she was late for their assignation?"

"The assignation she wasn't aware of because she hadn't arranged it?"

"Could be, Barnesy, could be - all these things are still possible."

"According to everyone's statements there was nobody else around at that time."

"Lady Bunny would have been in the lounge, but the curtains were closed tight according to Fairfax, so she wouldn't have been able to see him."

"Wait - when did Fairfax go for the tonic? Wasn't that around 10:40? Perhaps Edward Pritchard was waiting for Bunny Johnson and just happened to be looking upwards when Eleanor saw him? What if Edward Pritchard was waiting to see Bunny Johnson?"

"That's a good thought, Sergeant. She gets rid of Fairfax - having insufficient tonic is so convenient in this place - and speaks to Pritchard through the window, perhaps arranging to see him later, before Fairfax comes back. Don't forget Fairfax said she was wearing her cardigan when he came back, so that could have been why she became cold - opening the window to speak to Pritchard - if only Eleanor had waited a few more seconds when she went to see who was standing outside the Hall last night. Anyway, let's head over to St Anthony's in Manton Rempville village and find out when their bells were being rung last night by those campanologists. Then we should go to the Hart and have a bite to eat - I am starving. Let's hope Erin Beard is serving."

"I don't care who's serving, sir, I could eat a horse. Or a Shetland pony at least."

Barnes unlocked his Morgan and they got in.

"Are you concerned about anyone's safety, sir?" enquired Barnes as Knowles looked bemusedly at the topiary once again as the car headed down the drive.

"Well, I am, but I am not sure why. I am concerned that either Timmy Beauregard is spying on us or someone wants us to believe that he is - why would anyone want us to believe that? What threat is he to anyone?"

"He's one of those people who notices things, sir - he notices you saying that the murder took place at 11:06, when it appears other people didn't listen. If he was spying on us, perhaps he spied on other people too, such as the murderer?"

"Yes, you're right - he did notice the time. Maybe he knew the murder couldn't have been committed at that time? I am also worried about Miss Newton as she has been extremely helpful to us. I hope she doesn't tell other people what she told us - she could be in danger for that reason alone."

"So, there's St Anthony's church, sir, I wonder if there will be anyone in?"

"I am sure we would find God if we waited long enough, Sergeant."

"How reliable would his testament be in court?"

"I wouldn't use his testament, either the Old or the New, in court, Barnesy. God has proved to be an unreliable witness in the past, failing to show up on many occasions."

"You've called him have you, sir?"

"Thought about it - I have thought that it would be useful to have him contradict a defendant who keeps saying 'God spoke to me,' 'God made me do it.' Just to have this big booming voice say, 'it wasn't me - he's making it up.' Anyway, let's see who we can find in the house of God."

The two officers walked through the lych gate and across to the entrance. According to the notice board just outside the door, there was an active group of bell-ringers at the church, who were looking for more volunteers. There was a phone number for Reg Docherty, who was the leader of the team. Knowles went inside the church and looked around while Barnes phoned Mr. Docherty.

Knowles tucked in his shirt when he heard someone coming from the vestry. The Reverend Martin was a slim man aged about thirty-five, who had been the vicar at St Anthony's church for three years. He was the same height as Knowles and had short black hair.

"Hello, Reverend Martin, my name is Detective Inspector Colin Knowles from Scoresby CID," Knowles showed the Reverend his identity, "and I have a question about your bell-ringers."

"You wish to join them, Inspector?"

"Not yet, but you never know what might happen when I have solved the murder case I am working on at the moment."

"I see - and who has been murdered, Inspector?"

"A man named Edward Pritchard, who used to work at Manton Rempville Hall as a gardener; he was found dead in the monastery earlier today."

The Reverend Martin raised his eyebrows with surprise.

"That's terrible news; I used to see him around the village. He seemed very popular with everybody."

"Well that didn't extend to one particular person, who did away with him with a sword through the back."

"How grisly - do you feel one of the bell-ringers might have done it?"

"I don't think so, Reverend Martin, but I was wondering what time they were ringing until last night?"

"Practice on Friday lasts until 10:30p.m., Inspector, as do all practices throughout the week whenever they are held."

"It couldn't have run over last night, could it, until 10:40? Or even later?"

"No, Inspector Knowles, 10:30 is the limit - if it goes a second over I will receive an irate phone call from Mr. Grimshaw, who lives next to the church."

"And you received no irate phone calls last night then? Could Mr. Grimshaw be away?"

"Mr. Grimshaw isn't away and there were no calls last night."

At that moment, Sergeant Barnes came into the church and headed for the two men.

"This is my Sergeant, DS Rod Barnes, Reverend Martin. Barnesy, meet the vicar."

Sergeant Barnes and the Reverend Martin shook hands.

"So, what did you find out from Reg the bell-ringer, Sergeant?"

"I found out from Reg the bell-ringer that they actually finished slightly early last night, sir, at around 10:25."

"10:25? That's not what I was hoping to hear. Well, that corroborates what the Reverend told me."

"Back to the drawing board, perhaps?" said Reverend Martin, who almost seemed perturbed by the deflation that emanated so visibly from Knowles.

"Well, we shall have to carefully re-read everything that we were told and come up with another plausible explanation, won't we?" said Knowles trying to sound positive.

Barnes nodded and wondered what that explanation might be. Couldn't anyone at the Hall read the time properly - had everyone had their timepieces altered by the murderer?

"Well, thank you for your time, Reverend Martin. If I have any more questions I will let you know."

"It was a pleasure to meet you both and I hope you will consider ringing the bells here at St Anthony's in the future."

Knowles smiled and led Barnes out of the church with some alacrity. Once outside, Knowles looked up at the sky.

"I need a drink, Barnesy. There can only be one possible

explanation, which is that there's a second set of bells from somewhere like St Timothy's at Goat Parva or St Aidan's at Flixton or maybe both places."

"I thought everyone said they heard the bells from St Anthony's?"

"Not everyone did. Someone wanted to divert our attention from the truth by telling us where the bells were coming from, when in fact they weren't. Which sneaky bastard did that?"

"We'll have to go back through our notes and check."

"I know we will. Who was it who first mentioned the bells of St Anthony's? I can't remember."

"I think it might have been you, sir!"

"Really? Yes, you might be correct. Me and my big mouth."

"Anyway, should we head to the Hart at Norton and see if Erin Beard is there?"

"Absolutely, Sergeant, I am going to have their shepherd's pie and at least one pint of their best bitter. And talk to Beardy of course, if she's there - we need her to provide someone with an alibi for last night."

=========

Knowles was as good as his word when he arrived at the Hart and ordered a pint for Barnes, plus cod and chips, which was his Sergeant's favourite meal. He'd asked the landlord whether Erin Beard could come over and see them when she was on her break as he needed to talk to her.

Knowles and Barnes discussed the case and the plans for tomorrow.

"So, Barnesy, could you head over to Edward Pritchard's place first thing and see what you can find in his email inbox? I'd like to know who he thought he was going to be meeting last night. That should narrow it down somewhat. If he was expecting to meet Gwendoline then Ellis becomes prime suspect, at least in my humble opinion. If he thought he was meeting Bunny, then Sir Michael comes to the top of the list."

"And where will you be heading, sir?"

"Well, Sergeant, I will be going through those statements and my notes to see if I can glean any useful information. I will also try to find us another set of bells that were still ringing after 10:25p.m. Which direction was the wind coming from last night? Any ideas?"

"It's usually the south-west, isn't it?"

"I wonder if it was because there's no church for miles in that direction. The closest ones are due east of the Hall, which would explain why people heard them clearly."

"You mean people were hearing those bells all evening rather than St Anthony's because they would have been carried away on the wind?"

"Precisely, Sergeant Barnes, but we need to know the wind direction last night."

"I'll just look it up on my android phone," said Barnes, flashing his device in Knowles' direction. "I'll just search for the wind direction last night at this precise location and see what comes back... Well, there we are... Twenty miles an hour from the south-east until about 11:00p.m. and then it gradually veered to be a southerly gale."

"Everything is available at the touch of a screen, isn't it?" said Knowles, folding his arms as he felt uncomfortable discussing modern technology.

"That's a fair point, Inspector, because we didn't find any phone on the body, did we?" Barnes tapped the side of his head in self-mockery.

"We didn't, Sergeant - would you have expected to?"

"I would, if he was expecting to meet someone, he should have been contactable at the monastery, don't you think?" Barnes leaned forward on the table.

"Yes, I think you're right, so I will have to ask WPC Smythe to find his phone records and see who was in contact with him yesterday." Knowles got out a pen and wrote a reminder on the beermat.

"My guess would be no one was in contact with Pritchard yesterday, as that's a big clue to the murderer, isn't it, and our murderer is rather clever I fear."

"They might have made a mistake, Barnesy, and we'll

just have to find out what it is and seize the opportunity."

Barnes stood up and wiggled his empty glass at Knowles, who indicated he would like another pint thank you very much.

As Barnes headed towards the bar, a blonde woman of around thirty came the other way. Wearing a faded pair of jeans and a green T-shirt with 'Cuba' written in black across it, Erin Beard was beginning her break from serving at the bar and, rather than heading outside to chain smoke three cigarettes, she had been told by her boss to go and speak nicely to the policeman sitting under the horse brasses.

She sat down opposite Knowles and looked at him rather sullenly:

"You wanted to speak to me, Detective?"

Knowles feigned great pleasure.

"Erin - how are you and how is the import business?"

"Don't know what you mean, Detective, do you mind getting to the point?"

"Ah I see, got a packet of twenty you need to smoke in the next ten minutes, have you? It's alright, Erin, I am not here about your chain smoking habit and the consumption of tobacco at Olympic levels, I am here about last night. Was Sir Michael Johnson's son in here?"

"Yes, Cedric was definitely here for an hour or so, 'round about 9:30p.m., but I didn't see him much 'cos it was busy and I only had time to serve and not to chatter."

"Did he have any friends with him, do you remember?"

"I do remember, he had about three or four friends with him, for most of the time he was here."

"Three or four, you mean some left and then came back?"

"Possibly, I keep moving around, so sometimes you miss people because they're not in your line of sight."

"And they left around 10:30 to 10:40 you think?"

"It was around that time. The place was full to overflowing, so you can't always tell who's around and who's left."

"I suppose not. Well, thanks, Erin, I will leave you to your addiction; you're going to be a drain on the health service in the future, you know that, don't you?"

"If you say so, Detective."

With that, Erin Beard rose and went outside to smoke two cigarettes in the remaining few minutes of her break.

Barnes soon came back with a pint and a half of best bitter. He placed the drinks on the table and sat down.

"So what do you think's going to happen next, Inspector?" he asked, sipping the half.

"I think tomorrow will be a quiet day. You'll find some incriminating communications on Pritchard's computer, which will point us towards the murderer, and the case will be resolved to everyone's satisfaction."

Knowles' prediction couldn't have been further from the truth.

Chapter 4

Sunday 7:30a.m.

Colin Knowles was lying on a beach in the Caribbean. He was drinking a mojito and soaking up the rays of the sun, while secretly admiring some of the local females. Slowly the eloquent cawing of the parrots in the trees turned into the ringing of his phone and intruded into his dream. Knowles tried to find the device without opening his eyes, but only succeeded in knocking his mint tea on to the floor. Eventually he located the phone and drew it slowly to his left ear.

"'Allo, who is this? It had better be good."

Sergeant Rod Barnes gave Knowles a very good and brief reason why Knowles should come back from his reveries in the Caribbean to the realities of Manton Rempville Hall.

"When was this reported, Barnesy?" asked Knowles, checking the floor to see whether his tea had stained the carpet.

"Around 7:15a.m. by Fairfax," replied Barnes.

"And everyone else will know because of the ambulance sirens, I suppose," said Knowles, soaking up the excess tea with his bedside tissues.

"Yes, it was the first thing that Bunny Johnson mentioned to me - I am not convinced she is completely in touch with reality; sirens only after midday, what a ludicrous idea."

"What was the weapon that was used by the way; it wasn't the missing dagger, was it?"

"Kitchen knife, sir, straight out of the drawer."

"Someone is taking the mickey out of us, Sergeant Barnes, unless this is the thief's work and not the first murderer's work."

"That's getting very complicated, Inspector, having one killer is bad enough, but the thought there's competing murderers here is mind-boggling."

"Indeed it is, Sergeant - I will be over in thirty minutes. Keep everyone happy until I arrive."

"I will do my best, sir, I will do my best."

========

Knowles put two rounds of rye bread in his toaster and took the low-fat cream cheese out of his fridge. Freddie the cat was miaowing his head off and circling around Knowles' feet like a shark scenting blood. Knowles fed both cats from the can in the fridge door compartment. He ate his toasted bread and watched in amusement as Freddie gulped down his own food and then tried to eat Gemma's too. Gemma hissed and Freddie retreated under Knowles' chair, watching carefully until she had finished before daring to see whether there was anything left for him.

"You're out of luck, Freddie old son, she's finished everything," said Knowles as Freddie looked glumly in his direction. Knowles finished his toasted rye and put the plate with the crumbs on the floor for Freddie to lick voraciously.

Knowles brushed his teeth and put on his warm coat before exiting his house. The journey over to Manton Rempville Hall took ten minutes on a Sunday morning and he was soon heading down the drive towards the inexplicable topiary boxes. He saw Barnes standing in the turning circle with his hands on his hips. As Knowles brought his Land Rover to a halt, Barnes headed towards him.

"Now then, Barnesy, how bad is it?"

"Very clinical, sir, not brutal, but would have been instantaneous. The knife was pushed into the throat with force when the victim was asleep."

"Right, let's go and have a look." The officers headed towards the coach house and climbed the stairs. All the other guests were in the Hall and the only people present were from the Forensics team. The ambulance had left once the death had been confirmed.

Knowles greeted Dr. Crabtree.

"Well, Kevin, we should really meet under nicer circumstances occasionally."

Dr. Crabtree smiled and nodded in agreement.

"Indeed we should – oh, by the way, there was some dirt on the bottom of the handle of the sword, only a few faint specks but we found them…"

Knowles beamed, but indicated Dr. Crabtree should continue.

"…Anyway, the victim is Basil Fawcett and he has been neatly stabbed through the throat with a large kitchen knife, used for carving meat. No fingerprints at all, which suggests the killer cleaned the handle at some point. Basil would not have known a thing. He would not have made a noise. I understand Toby was in the next room and Henrietta was down the hallway. Both are distraught and are receiving counselling. Time of death around seven hours ago, approximately 1:30a.m."

Knowles looked down at Basil and shook his head.

"Oh, Basil, you didn't tell us something - what did you do when Toby and Henrietta went for their walk? Who did you see - who was outside the lower study window at 11:30p.m. - did you follow them and didn't tell us?"

"Does this mean he saw the murderer or Edward Pritchard before he was killed?" asked Barnes.

"Unless this is a random attack then yes, I think it does mean that - I think we can safely say that Edward Pritchard was killed after 11:30p.m. and that his watch was smashed to give the murderer an alibi. Perhaps Pritchard was the figure outside the lower study that Basil saw."

"Why can't people just be totally open with us, sir?" asked Barnes almost beseechingly.

"Maybe Basil here was trying a little blackmail with the murderer?"

"But he had no guile, did he? Just think about how he hung around outside the interview room door and you saw his reflection in the window. He was genuinely surprised you'd seen him. Very naive."

"Is there anything in his pockets or on his phone that we could use, such as a text or a phone number?"

"His phone has a passcode, which isn't immediately obvious and his pockets revealed nothing."

"Not immediately obvious, what does that mean?"

"Well, it's not B-A-S-I-L, 12345, or 54321, for example."

"Does his sister know his passcode?"

"She might, but she's too upset right now, not surprisingly."

Knowles nodded thoughtfully. He hoped that the phone would reveal some significant communication between Basil and the person who had murdered him.

"So, Barnesy, why did Fairfax find the body and not Henrietta or Toby?"

"He was rousing people for a planned trip to the golf course, which Basil had expressed an interest in. 8:30a.m. tee off time, apparently."

"And Henrietta and Toby weren't going?"

"Apparently not, sir."

"I wonder if we shouldn't go and look at Pritchard's place and then come back here when everyone's had a chance to eat breakfast and to absorb the news. I doubt that Henrietta would be in any fit state to answer our questions now, anyway."

"That sounds like a plan, sir, and I would agree with you regarding Henrietta."

"Thought you might, Barnesy."

"Shall we go then? I will go and tell Sir Michael that we will be back in a couple of hours."

"Sounds good, Sergeant, I will see you by the vehicles in a couple of minutes."

Barnes smiled and left the room.

Knowles turned to Dr. Crabtree.

"Was there any sign of a struggle, at all?"

"None whatsoever, Colin, he was taken completely by surprise by the looks of it."

"Nothing under the nails?"

"Nothing at all."

"Right, well would you say the person who did this committed the first murder too?"

"It's likely; don't forget this killing was more surgical than the first and the knife was inserted from above into the throat really quickly."

"And the place it was inserted suggests prior knowledge of how to kill people quickly?"

"No, not really, I couldn't say that - the throat is the most vulnerable part of the anatomy if you're in bed and your attacker has a knife. And that might be a clue because a strong man would have smothered Basil with a pillow."

"There'd be noise though, Kevin, with a pillow and a struggle too, both of which might have woken up the neighbours."

"I suppose so, Colin. Anyway, can we take the body away now?"

"Please do, Kevin."

Dr. Crabtree's assistant, who'd been hovering in the background, came forward and helped the doctor move the body on to the stretcher. The photographer took some pictures of the now empty bedclothes as Basil Fawcett began his last but one journey to the morgue at Scoresby police station.

Knowles followed at a respectful distance before telling one of the constables in the courtyard to guard Basil's room until he and Barnes came back.

Knowles and Barnes climbed into Barnes' sports car.

"Wow, I actually fit in the seat now," said Knowles, "and I don't feel like I am flowing over the edges. This diet's working really well."

"You have to keep it up, sir, keep up the lifestyles, keep up the exercise, keep up the healthy eating."

"Yes, that's what I tell myself every morning, Sergeant. Anyway, I feel a bit odd leaving all those people together in a confined space knowing that one of them might have killed two people in cold blood."

"So you think it was the same killer? You don't think this was the original thief killing his victim with the first sharp implement he could lay his hands on?"

"Our murderer has a penchant for sharp knives and I was expecting the ceremonial dagger to be used, however that's being saved for later by the looks of it."

"Saved, that's a bit worrying, isn't it, sir?"

"It is, Barnesy, which is why I feel odd leaving them all

together, but I doubt anything will happen in broad daylight."

"At Pritchard's place, we should try and find his phone and see who he was communicating with."

"I would guess that his phone will be missing and might even have been used by the murderer to communicate with our recently departed Basil."

"That would only work if Basil knew Pritchard's number; it's hard to believe the murderer would have contacted Basil initially, isn't it?"

"Unless Basil's number was on Pritchard's phone, which is a bit suspicious in the first place, but let's just play this through. Why would Basil suspect that the murderer had Pritchard's phone? The only answer can be that he saw the murderer take the phone. So, Sergeant, Basil sees the murder and then blackmails the murderer, who still has the phone."

"Why would the murderer take the phone though, sir?"

"For some information on the phone, an email, a text, a photo perhaps, some kind of evidence that the murderer could use."

"Evidence of what though?"

"We find that out, we find our murderer, Sergeant, I can almost guarantee it."

"What was the number on this street?"

"Number 4."

The houses on Durham Street were narrow but just about detached from each other, allowing the occupants to squeeze between neighbouring properties. Pritchard's garden was well stocked with conifers and low-maintenance bushes. Dotted in between were splashes of bright colour including begonias, nerines, sternbergia, and cyclamens.

"Gemma would like this garden; plenty of places to secrete yourself from the local bird and vole population."

"Wouldn't catch a dog doing such a sneaky thing," quipped Barnes.

Knowles almost replied, but held his tongue. Sergeant Barnes was developing a nice, ironic sense of humour, which had to be carefully nurtured. Knowles smiled to no one in particular and looked at the front door.

"It's nice to see that young Edward kept his garden in

good nick; I wonder if any of these plants came from Manton Rempville Hall?"

"We should ask Jenkins."

"I am not sure he would give an answer other than 'yes', Sergeant; he's not exactly impartial."

"You think he was the one who stole the plants?"

"I am not here to assess who the plant thief is, Barnesy, I am here to investigate the home of a murder victim. If that victim has been battered with a bunch of begonias then perhaps the identity of the plant thief might be of great interest. Shall we go inside and see what we can find?"

The blue front door had been recently painted and the brass letter box polished. Barnes took out the keys that had been found on Pritchard's body and tried two keys in the lock before the third opened the door. There were a couple of bills on the mat, which Knowles placed on the hallway table.

"So what's the plan, sir?"

"You take the upstairs and I'll take a look around here and see if there's anything suspicious. Don't forget we could do with finding his mobile phone and accessing the email on his home computer, if he has one."

Barnes nodded and headed up the stairs. Knowles looked around the entrance hall and noted the absence of indoor plants, a theme which continued in the lounge and dining room. There was a large mirror hanging over the ornamental fireplace and a copy of Munch's 'The Scream' on the wall opposite. Knowles mimicked the face in the poster and then wondered whether that's how Pritchard felt when the sword killed him.

Knowles looked into the kitchen and noted the single plate and cup in the dish rack. The knife and fork were still in the sink although they had been washed. One of the tea towels was on the floor and the coffee maker was still on although the coffee had been drunk. He looked in the cupboards and saw that the tins were lined up in neat rows. Some loose flour had been clipped tightly closed with a bulldog clip.

"Obviously a neat and tidy person in the kitchen at least," thought Knowles as he admired the interior of the fridge. A

half-full bottle of white wine had pride of place on the middle shelf along with a fine piece of Red Leicester. Various types of yoghourt filled the shelves along with fruit juice, soy milk, and free-range eggs.

"There's absolutely nothing suspicious here," said Knowles to himself, "which is a bit strange."

Knowles walked back to the hall and climbed the stairs to find Barnes. The walls were painted a light green colour and there were four posters on the walls from famous gardens in England. Barnes was in a kind of study room looking at the desktop computer.

"Well, Barnesy, there's absolutely nothing suspicious downstairs - what have you found on there?"

"Well, he didn't clear his history on the Internet, so I can tell you he likes gardening sites, soft porn, and sports such as football and rugby."

"Fairly normal for a young gardener then," replied Knowles, "and his email?"

"It's protected by a username and password, which aren't written down on a piece of paper on this desk. His bedroom's quite tidy and I think his mobile phone has been taken as the battery charger is on his bedside table."

"Any pictures on the table of his family or friends?"

"There's no pictures of women, if that's what you mean, but he has a picture of what must be his dad, I would guess, and perhaps a brother."

"Interesting information. Can you check his images on here and perhaps Photoshop too, to see whether he kept any digital images of his girlfriends?" Knowles had noticed that there was digital SLR on one of the shelves in the room along with some photography books and a camera bag.

"Will do, sir, Photoshop is always a good place to start as people do like to try and improve their own images. Photoshop is just opening now. We'll be able to see where his most recent images were stored. Right, here we are - it looks like they were stored on a DVD, which is still in the drive. Let's hope they're not pictures of flowers and trees."

The first image, which had last been updated two days previously, was of Gwendoline. She was smiling and holding a plant stalk between her teeth in a coquettish sort of way. She looked very happy and beautiful, even without any noticeable make-up. The next three images were also of Gwendoline, but the one after that was of Bunny Johnson, who was also smiling but in a more furtive way. She looked nervous, as though she really didn't want to be photographed.

"So there was something going on between them," said Barnes.

"Well, one photo doesn't prove anything, Sergeant, and she does look nervous about things."

Three more images of Bunny Johnson appeared and then one of Henrietta Fawcett.

Barnes shook his head as he displayed three more images of Henrietta.

"These are close up photos, so she knew she was being photographed; they're not taken from a distance through a long lens," he said.

"That's right, Barnesy, I hope you're not too disappointed."

"I am, actually, but not surprised as she is extremely lovely. Does this give her a reason to kill Pritchard?"

"It might do; some kind of youthful anger perhaps, but she was with Toby don't forget and they were together the whole time. They were close to the murder scene at the time we think Pritchard was killed, around 11:40p.m., but they told us they didn't see anything."

"They could have been lying, I suppose, Inspector?"

"They could, Sergeant, but I don't think Toby would cover for Henrietta being out of his sight for a few minutes."

"He would ask her where she'd been."

"He would, of course he would, I would have."

"He would have told us, wouldn't he, sir?"

"You would hope so, I would have."

"It couldn't have slipped his mind?"

"I hope not, otherwise we are in trouble with the investigation."

"But wait, if Henrietta and Toby were apart, perhaps Basil saw this and yet when he spoke to them, they said that they hadn't told us about this separation. Basil was guileless and his face would have given the game away. Henrietta and Toby now know that Basil saw them when they separated and so neither of them has an alibi and could be the killer. Sure enough one of them is the killer and murders Basil before he can speak to us."

"Wait, you're suggesting that Henrietta killed her own brother or that Toby killed one of his best friends?"

"I am suggesting that as a possibility, sir."

"That is very imaginative, Sergeant Barnes, and does place two people back in the frame who had previously been discounted, by me at least." Knowles placed his hand on his chest to emphasize the point.

"Shall we see who else we have in the rogues gallery?"

"Yes, let's."

Images of Miss Newton, James Beauregard, Basil Fawcett and Mrs. Swarbrick came and went before the subject changed to flowers, of which there were many different types.

"When were these images taken, Barnesy?"

"I will just check the directory listing. It should show when they were taken."

As Barnes accessed the DVD drive, Knowles picked up the camera and scanned the images that were still on the camera's image card. They seemed to be mostly the same as the ones on the DVD. Knowles took out the card and placed it into a small plastic bag for evidence.

"According to these dates, those pictures were taken three months ago, which was presumably the last time everyone, apart from Timmy, was here together."

"He took a picture of James Beauregard; I wonder if that's why James fell for him, because Edward Pritchard took a picture of him. James assumed a lot."

"He also took two pictures of Miss Newton, who looked very relaxed about the whole thing. I wonder if Pritchard took the pictures all at once, such as at a picnic?"

"The times indicate all the images, apart from Gwendoline's, were taken within half an hour of each other. Gwendoline's were taken a couple of hours earlier."

"Were they now, well that's interesting - I thought she said she hadn't spoken to him for six months?"

"I suppose the months just merge into each other as you get older, Inspector."

"In my experience it's the years that do that, not the months."

"I didn't think you were that old, sir."

"I feel younger than I did five years ago, especially since losing the weight."

Barnes thought about agreeing with Knowles but decided against it as he might have come across as being sarcastic.

"I'll just make a note, sir, to ask Gwendoline about her faulty memory as regards meeting Pritchard three months ago."

"Take that DVD with you and print those pictures off back at the station - all the images of all the people, not just Gwendoline. And don't keep one of Henrietta for yourself, Barnesy."

"Actually, I wasn't going to print off any pictures for myself - I think Henrietta is not my type after all."

"You think she's the murdering type then?"

"She might be, but that would mean she killed her brother, wouldn't it?"

"Well, not necessarily, Barnesy - don't forget that I think the sword was stolen by a thief, but that the sword was purloined and used on Edward Pritchard by the murderer, so that the thief, the original thief if you like, may have been intending to commit murder but was thwarted by the murderer of Pritchard..."

Barnes was looking very confused.

"....No, bear with me, Basil might have been killed by the original thief and not by the murderer of Pritchard. There's that possibility too."

Barnes scratched his goatee beard and then spoke.

"So you think there might be two murderers, one of whom is pre-meditated and the other is more impulsive. Pritchard's is more interested in correcting the natural order of things by using a symbol of old family values to remove the upstart from the life of an established family. The other sees an

111

opportunity to kill a nosey parker, who has seen something he shouldn't have and uses the only implement that's readily available to him."

"Perhaps, and if you are correct then Basil didn't see the first murder but saw something, which made him dangerous to someone else."

"Could the two murderers be working together, do you think?"

"I don't believe so, Barnesy, that would be pushing things too far."

"And Basil wouldn't have murdered Edward Pritchard and then been killed himself? Could Basil have taken the sword after the original thief had relocated it in the tunnel?"

"Well, that's a good point because Basil doesn't have an alibi after 11:25p.m., does he? So perhaps he could have."

"How do we prove Basil took the sword from the passage on Friday night though, sir?"

"Well, Sergeant, by proving he killed Pritchard - he might have seen the original thief relocating the sword in the tunnel and taken the sword to kill Pritchard, although obviously Basil hadn't arranged to meet Pritchard. The thief must have arranged to meet Pritchard at the monastery and relocated the sword, but then he or she is beaten to it by Basil."

"That's possible and perhaps the thief saw Basil kill Pritchard and that's why Basil was killed."

"But why murder someone who's done your dirty work for you? It's the perfect murder - get someone else to do it. Why ever would you kill the person who's done what you were intending to do? That doesn't make any sense!" Barnes shook his head.

"There has to be a reason - perhaps the murderer thought that Basil would talk to us and indicate who had stolen the sword in the first place."

"So are we looking for two murderers then, sir?"

"It is possible, Sergeant, that Basil killed Edward Pritchard for reason or reasons unknown at this point. Perhaps Basil was then killed by the person who originally stole the sword and, who knows, perhaps that person also intended to kill Pritchard but was beaten to it by Basil?"

"Right, so we should pursue that line of enquiry too."

"Yes, I will phone WPC Smythe and ask her to take a counsellor to see Henrietta. We need to know what reason Basil would have had for killing Edward Pritchard on impulse. I am sure Henrietta will be expecting us to ask who would want to kill Basil, so she will be surprised at our questions. I'll ask Linda to obtain the phone records for Pritchard too."

"Sounds like a plan, sir - I will attach these images to an email and send them off to Forensics so they can print them off for us. I will keep the DVD with me."

"That's good, Sergeant, I'll phone Linda now and I will see you back at your vehicle, so we can drive back to the Hall. Don't forget to lock up."

Barnes smiled and set about sending the images. He lingered over the picture of Henrietta and wondered how she was feeling at the moment, given all that had happened in the past few hours. He examined the image of Basil Fawcett and wondered whether he was looking at the face of a murderer.

=========

Barnes and Knowles drove back to Manton Rempville Hall and were met by an anxious Fairfax, who appeared to have been waiting for them to arrive. As soon as Knowles stepped out of the car Fairfax spoke to him in a concerned manner.

"Sir Michael is most insistent the murderer be caught as soon as possible; he feels his reputation is being sullied by these terrible events."

Knowles almost smiled at the reasoning behind Sir Michael's anxiety, however Knowles decided to address his own main concern.

"I am concerned that the murderer be caught too as I don't want anyone else to lose their life. My Sergeant and I will be talking to certain people in a few minutes in order to establish what's happened and I hope people will start to tell the truth. A counsellor will be coming to speak with Henrietta and my WPC will also be there."

"I will convey your message to Sir Michael and I am sure he will be relieved to hear you and he share a common desire to catch the murderer."

"It is our job to do that," said Barnes who had been listening in, "we are always trying to catch the criminal."

"Of course it is, Sergeant," replied Fairfax, backing away slightly, "I am sure we all appreciate that." With that he turned around and headed into the Hall.

"Was that really necessary?" wondered Knowles. "Send your flunkey out to convey your 'concern' about catching the murderer as the publicity is affecting your chances of becoming the next MP for the area?"

"Absolutely - one can't have one's career as an MP being threatened by people going around stabbing other people with sharp, pointed objects."

"So who should we speak to first?"

"Well, Barnesy, I would like you to talk to Miss Newton and Mrs. Swarbrick about having their picture taken by Edward Pritchard and when this photographic event actually took place."

"Right, I'll ask Mrs. Swarbrick about the knife too although I would imagine there's probably a dozen in the kitchen like that one."

"Good idea, I will go and talk to Gwendoline about her faulty memory and why she had her photo taken separately from everyone else. I am looking forward to her replies. Once we've done that we should look in Basil's room for any clues."

As Knowles finished WPC Smythe drove up with the counsellor, Sue Perkins, who was going to talk to Henrietta about Basil.

"OK, Barnesy, you go and see Newton and Swarbrick and I will just talk to Sue here first."

Barnes nodded and headed off into the Hall to find the two servants.

Knowles turned around and greeted the two women.

"'Allo, Linda and Sue, I haven't seen you for ages, Sue, where've you been hiding - are you keeping out of my way?"

"I have been, Colin, quite successfully too, but you've finally smoked me out!"

"Indeed, and Linda, how are you?"

"Not looking forward to this, sir, I would expect Henrietta is going to be very upset when we talk to her."

"Well, Sue is going to be gauging how Henrietta is reacting to this tragedy, so you will have to take your cue from her, but what I would like you to do is ascertain the veracity of what Henrietta says regarding Basil's thoughts about Edward Pritchard."

"Henrietta's not going to be expecting that line of questioning, is she? That's going to be interesting," said Smythe.

"Do you really want me to broach that subject?" asked Perkins.

"If you can, yes, I have a suspicion that Basil might have killed Pritchard, you see, so any light that Henrietta could shed on Basil's opinions about Pritchard would be greatly appreciated. If you could also ask her what the password is on Basil's phone that would be excellent."

"Right, Colin, I will see what I can do, but the timing might not be right," replied Perkins.

"Understood, Sue, anyway let's go and find the people we want to speak to," said Knowles and motioned for the two women to follow him into the Hall.

Once inside Knowles saw Fairfax heading into the lower study with a cup of tea on a tray. Fairfax saw him and indicated he would be back in one minute.

When Fairfax returned he closed the study door behind him and held the tray in front of him almost like a shield.

"How can I help you, Inspector?"

"Well, the first thing is, where can I find Gwendoline?"

"Miss Johnson is in the lounge with Mr. Ellis."

"Thank you and the second and last question is, where is Henrietta Fawcett? These two ladies here would like to talk with her in private."

"My understanding is that she's lying down in her room."

"She's not on her own, is she?" interjected Sue Perkins.

"I think Master Toby might be with her."

"Right, please take WPC Smythe and Counsellor Perkins to Henrietta and bring Master Toby back with you, if you would, Mr. Fairfax."

"Of course, Inspector, ladies if you would like to follow me please?" said Fairfax and the three of them headed over to the coach house, leaving Knowles in the hallway wondering how he could remove Ellis Hardaker from the lounge so as to talk to Gwendoline in private.

Having thought of a suitable story, Knowles walked towards the play room only to be met by Gwendoline coming the other way. Her eyes were slightly moistened and Knowles wondered whether she and Ellis had been arguing.

"Hello, Gwendoline, are you available for a private chat?"

Gwendoline glanced behind her and said in a slightly louder voice than normal, "Of course, Inspector Knowles, shall we go outside and have a look around the gardens?"

Knowles shrugged his shoulders and said "OK." He looked towards the door of the play room, half expecting Ellis to come rushing out, but he didn't. By using a raised voice it seemed to Knowles as though Gwendoline was trying to warn Ellis, though Knowles couldn't work out why. Perhaps she was worried that Ellis was going to continue their argument outside the confines of the lounge?

By the time Knowles had done his thinking Gwendoline was almost outside and Knowles almost had to run to catch her up.

"Is everything fine between yourself and Ellis, Gwendoline?" asked Knowles.

"We have our ups and downs, Inspector, like most couples, and we've just had a bit of a down today regarding the murder of Edward on Friday. I was asking Ellis why he went out to the car on Friday night instead of staying in our bedroom and he didn't have a particularly good explanation, something about leaving his i-Pad in the car rather than bringing it up to the room."

"Perhaps he just plain forgot?"

"Ellis doesn't forget things like that, Inspector Knowles, he left it there to use it as an excuse to be out of the room - shall we go this way towards the monastery?"

"Why would he need an excuse to be out of the room?"

"He was sending emails about business that he didn't want me to see, for some reason."

"And you know he sent them?"

"He said he did and there'd be a record of them being sent, wouldn't there?"

"Perhaps we should obtain his i-Pad as evidence, just to see what was going on."

"Yes, that might be interesting, Inspector, you should do that,"

"Talking of what was going on, when we spoke to you yesterday you said you hadn't spoken to Edward Pritchard for six months and yet Sergeant Barnes and I saw a picture of you about an hour ago that was taken by Edward three months ago, when everyone last got together here at Manton Rempville Hall."

"He might have taken my picture at the same time as he took everyone else's picture at a picnic we had."

"The time your picture was taken was about two hours before everyone else's picture, which indicates that either it was a very long picnic or you did see him before the picnic."

"OK, I did speak to him before the picnic, briefly, and he did take my picture but unfortunately my father saw him and told him to go away. I think that was the final straw for my father and he fired Edward at the picnic, after everyone had eaten and all the pictures had been taken."

"That was very considerate of Sir Michael," said Knowles rather sarcastically.

"Yes, it was - my father's not usually that considerate."

"What did Pritchard talk to you about when he met you?" enquired Knowles.

"He pleaded with me to start seeing him again, but I told him that wasn't possible because I was as good as engaged to Ellis and that my parents would never accept him as anything other than a gardener. And then my father rather proved my point."

"So would Ellis have wanted to kill Edward Pritchard? Could your father have done it? Or what about someone like Basil Fawcett?"

Gwendoline sighed. "My father has immense ambition, starting with being an MP, so I doubt he would have jeopardised this ambition for a murder there was no need for. Edward Pritchard was no longer part of his life, why would he risk everything for someone who no longer mattered to him?"

"Could Edward have been blackmailing him with his pictures of either yourself or your mother?"

"My mother? Are you saying Edward Pritchard had some compromising pictures of my mother?"

"Perhaps he did - we've seen some pictures of her."

"Unbelievable, quite frankly, anyway you asked about Ellis – well, he does have a bad temper on occasions, but murdering someone would be beyond him, I think, especially with a sword in cold blood."

"Is he a bit squeamish then?"

"I think so; he cut his finger once and almost fainted."

"And what about Basil Fawcett?"

"Basil who has just been murdered? Basil murder someone? Well you can never tell, can you, but what would his motive have been? He would have only have known Edward from the previous weekend three months ago and would only have met him briefly, so Basil would not be top of the list of my suspects."

"You have a list of suspects for the murder of Edward Pritchard?"

"It's more of a list of non-suspects as I can't see one of the family doing it, so I could only think of perhaps Wilkinson or more likely Jenkins who would have wanted to kill Edward."

"Why would they have wanted to do that - what would have been their motives?" enquired Knowles.

"Well, someone spread a rumour about Wilkinson and Mrs. Swarbrick having an affair and Edward was blamed for that. Jenkins might have been stealing the flowers and not Edward. Jenkins might have wanted to stop Edward telling my father the truth." Gwendoline wiped a tear away.

"Right, I have heard enough of this what I believe is called obfuscation in legal terms," said Knowles quite harshly, "Edward Pritchard would never dare approach your father because your father despised Pritchard and wouldn't believe a word he said, so the idea that Jenkins would be concerned that your father would even listen to Pritchard is quite frankly preposterous. You are not telling me the whole truth, Gwendoline. You suspect someone; you told us that in our private interview yesterday, someone had said something that had alerted you to another person's feelings about Pritchard. Are you trying to tell me that this third person was Jenkins?"

"Yes, Inspector, I am telling you that but it is only hearsay. The intimation was that Jenkins was stealing plants and pinned the blame successfully on Edward, but Edward had some proof that it was Jenkins who was stealing them and selling them in Northamptonshire. I think Edward looked on Jenkins' computer when he'd left it switched on once and found some email from the buyer, so he was hoping to use that as evidence to try and get his job back by blackmailing Jenkins to put in a good word for him with my father. But I don't think Jenkins kept his word and he killed Edward in order to shut him up."

"How many people was Edward blackmailing or attempting to blackmail?" asked Knowles.

"I am sure I have no idea," replied Gwendoline looking offended.

"He never told you or even bragged about it?"

"We weren't that close, Inspector Knowles, but I do know that Edward wouldn't brag and certainly not about his own desperate attempts to obtain money from others. Anyway, I would like to turn back towards the Hall now as I don't really feel this conversation has helped."

"But you've just mentioned Wilkinson and Jenkins. How about your mother? Did Pritchard have any hold over her, for example? Is that why everyone was invited back again?"

"Inspector Knowles, my mother let Edward get too close to her and she deeply regrets allowing this to happen, but I am sure he wasn't blackmailing her. He might have persuaded her to invite everyone back again in a misguided attempt to clear his name in front of us all."

"You think he spoke to your mother after he was banned from the property?"

"I think he might have been outside the Hall on the monastery side near the lounge windows around 11:20p.m. on Friday night. I did glance through the curtains at one point and I thought I saw him. I might have been wrong, Inspector."

"And who would he have been waiting for, do you think?" enquired Knowles,

"Well, to be truthful, I had a fleeting belief that he might have been waiting for Ellis."

"Why would you believe that, Gwendoline?"

"Well, Ellis' excuse of leaving his i-Pad in the car didn't seem plausible to me and I know he still resented Edward for his previous interest in me."

"But who would have initiated the meeting; how would either of them have contacted the other? Did you provide contact details? Email? Phone number?" Knowles was really trying not to show his irritation, but he knew he might be failing miserably.

"I didn't provide either of them with 'contact details' as you put it, Inspector, I was always worried there would be trouble if the two of them met on their own."

"But you intimated Ellis wasn't a violent person?"

Gwendoline stopped walking because the two of them were close to the house now.

"Inspector Knowles, Ellis Hardaker isn't violent but he is passionate about me and who knows how people will behave when they are placed in certain situations where those passions can be excited."

"I know what you're saying - my maternal grandfather never said much and hardly showed his emotions, but he was passionate about his racing pigeons. One day his pigeon, Blue Bobby, won one of the big races up north and he shouted and danced around for a minute in his excitement."

"Well, congratulations to him, what happened next - did he go back to being stoical?"

"No, not really, he clutched at his chest and dropped dead from a heart attack."

There was an awkward silence.

"I am sorry to hear about your maternal grandfather, Inspector."

"Yes, we all were, Gwendoline. The point is that none of us had ever seen him act like that before, at least not in public. He surprised us all."

"I see, yes, that's interesting as a comparison."

"Ellis meeting Edward is plausible; it's the arranging of the meeting that causes me to doubt it actually happened. Anyway, I should go and see my Sergeant - he's hovering over there like a fat vulture."

"What do you mean?"

"A fat vulture would have great difficulty in hovering and would have to put a lot of effort into it and look awkward too, and that's how Sergeant Barnes looks now, I feel. I should go and help him out."

Gwendoline smiled and thanked Knowles for their conversation. Knowles returned the compliment before walking over to Barnes who was standing outside the lower study.

"O what can ail thee, knight-at-arms, alone and palely loitering?" enquired Knowles.

"I'm fine, sir, thanks for asking."

"It's Keats, Sergeant, the opening lines of *La Belle Dame sans Merci.*"

"Is that a poem?"

"It is, Sergeant Barnes, what a good guess."

"And it means the beautiful woman without a thank you?"

"That's half correct."

"Was she a prostitute?"

"More of a femme fatale, but you're getting the right idea. Anyway, speaking of femme fatales, how were Mrs. Swarbrick and Miss Newton?"

"Well, they were... what's the correct term - surprised and disappointed I think - that their pictures had been kept by Edward Pritchard, and neither of them remember him taking their pictures, so it's possible that someone else took those images using Pritchard's camera at the picnic."

"That's not completely unusual, is it?"

"At a social event, no it's not."

"I wonder who took those pictures then?"

"I don't know and neither of the ladies could remember, but whoever it was didn't tell them that Pritchard's camera was being used, otherwise they probably would have refused."

"I see, Barnesy, perhaps some people did know, which is why not everyone's picture was on the DVD."

"Perhaps, sir, it's possible - should we go and see Basil's room now?"

"Yes, let's see if we can find any evidence to see who might have murdered him in such a terrible manner."

========

As they walked over to the coach house Knowles recounted his conversation with Gwendoline to Barnes and how she had indicated that Pritchard might have been waiting to meet Ellis Hardaker. Barnes wondered how that meeting could have been arranged and Knowles replied that neither he nor Gwendoline had come up with a plausible explanation.

Both policeman smiled at the constable at the entrance to the coach house and then headed upstairs to Basil Fawcett's room. The room had been left by the Forensics team as they had found it a few hours earlier apart from the bed, which had been stripped of its blankets and sheets.

"So do you want to look in his suitcase and hold-all?" asked Knowles, "I will look in the cupboard, under the bed, and in the bathroom."

"Sounds like a plan, sir," said Barnes, heading over to the green Delsey suitcase, which was lying closed on the floor. He pressed the side locks, which sprang open and then pressed the small yellow panel in the main, central lock. This released and he gently opened the suitcase and let the lid lie against the wall. He looked inside and saw two pairs of socks, which had been neatly folded together. There was also a plastic bag containing Basil's dirty washing from the previous two days - jockey shorts, socks, and a T-shirt. Underneath the bag was a travel iron and a small pouch of medical supplies including aspirins and antacid tablets. He took out his pen and used it to open slightly the two side pockets, made from material, so that he could peer inside each. One of these pockets contained some razor blades and a spare toothbrush.

The pocket on the inner lid of the suitcase revealed some objects of more interest. An opened pack of ten condoms caught his attention as did a half bottle of whisky that was a quarter full. There were various baggage tags indicating Basil had been to Barbados, Dubai, and Cairo. Barnes unhooked the inner lid and wasn't too surprised to find some soft porn magazines come sliding into view. Hidden amongst them, however, was a copy of *Practical Hunting Blade* magazine. Barnes glanced through the pages with a certain amount of disbelief. He had this strange feeling that he was meant to find this magazine and he was glad that he'd remembered to put on gloves before starting the search.

"Sir, what kind of magazines do you think I've found in Basil Fawcett's suitcase?"

"Pornographic magazines, I would imagine," said Knowles from inside the en-suite bathroom.

"Any others?"

Knowles stuck his head around the bathroom door and said: "Is there a magazine called *Cavalry Sword Weekly* or *How to Murder in a Monastery*?"

"There might be, but I have in my hand *Practical Hunting Blade* magazine and it feels like I was meant to find this, if you know what I am getting at?"

"It's a plant, you mean?"

"Yes, it looks like it - I will place this in an evidence bag and see whose paw prints we can find on it."

"And more importantly, whether Basil's paw prints are on any of the pages."

"I will throw in one of the porn mags too as these are really well thumbed and will surely give a match for Basil's fingerprints."

"Good idea, Barnesy, that way, you can be sure that Forensics will put your request to the top of their list - you will have their undivided attention."

"I didn't know Sally was interested in porn."

"She's interested in the practice rather than looking - there's a tip for you, Sergeant - but sadly for you and your libido she's away in Jamaica for two weeks, so your request will be looked after by lecher McNair."

"Just my luck, she's a sure thing is she?"

"Well, there's no accounting for taste is there, but sometimes the queue for her at office parties is longer than the queue for the buffet."

"The buffets are terrible though, sir, that's not saying much. I thought she was raising money for charity by giving kisses under the mistletoe?"

"While the Chief Inspector's there, yes, that's true, but afterwards... Anyway, get on with your search in the hold-all, Sergeant Barnes."

"Yes, sir," said Barnes giving a mock salute, before adding, "Have you found anything?"

"Yes, tea-tree flavoured toothpaste which tastes really good actually, I will have to take some for Gemma. Nothing else unusual to report."

Barnes laughed and started to examine the hold-all. Inside, he found a small umbrella and half-a-dozen golf balls still in their plastic wrapping. There was also a glove, two thin jumpers, and a full set of waterproofs.

"Looks like Basil was intending to play golf as Fairfax indicated to you, sir, he seems to have been taking it quite seriously."

"He didn't bring any clubs with him though, did he?" replied Knowles.

"Not unless they're in Toby's car. Fairfax didn't say that he had already taken them before trying to rouse Basil, but then again I didn't ask him."

"You wouldn't do, but when we've finished searching go and ask him."

"Are you thinking what I'm thinking, sir?"

"What, that a golf bag would be a good place to hide a sword?"

"Yes."

"That thought did cross my mind; it would only work if

he played golf, and brought his clubs with him, the last time he was up here for the weekend." Knowles frowned when he realised what this might mean for all his current theories about the murders.

"Indeed it would, Inspector, I will ask Fairfax that too," said Barnes, replacing the items into the hold-all with great difficulty - it reminded him of packing his suitcase when returning from his holidays. The belongings just wouldn't fit.

"Have you looked in the cupboards, Inspector?"

"Not yet, no, if you want to look go ahead, I won't be offended," said Knowles, who was now on his knees scanning under the bed. "Have you noticed something, Barnesy, there's no sign of dirt on this carpet. None whatsoever. Now, does this mean that the murderer took off his shoes before entering the room or did he change into slippers before coming in…?"

"Or maybe the murderer didn't come from the outside…"

"Yes, perhaps, you see Basil's shoes are all by the door - very neat and tidy, very admirable, so any dirt would have come from the murderer's shoes as these rooms are cleaned daily, but there's nothing."

"I should check by the front door and see if there's any sign of shoes. That would be the best place for the murderer to remove footwear as there's an outside light, which is always on as far as I can tell."

"Sounds risky to me, lingering under a light, I think it's more likely they had a torch, but go and check both doors now just in case the cleaner wants to start tidying up."

"Will do, sir, and I will go and ask Fairfax about Basil and his golf."

Barnes left the room and Knowles continued looking under the bed and in the cupboards. Basil enjoyed wearing bright colours and three of his shirts and three pairs of trousers were all ironed carefully. Three T-shirts and various items of underwear were arranged with great precision in a drawer.

Knowles smiled and checked the suitcase again. He then made a call to Forensics at Scoresby station and asked them to kindly return to the coach house at Manton Rempville Hall as he had something of interest for them to analyse.

=========

While Knowles was on the phone, Barnes was inspecting the area around the front door of the coach house. He was thankful that Knowles and himself had placed plastic covers over their shoes before entering the building. Methodical police work solved more cases than flashes of blind inspiration, despite what TV programmes would have you believe.

Barnes stared at the floor and tried to see the outlines of a pair of shoes but couldn't make them appear. Likewise at the back door, even though this was less surprising as the door was bolted on the inside and was only intended for use in emergencies.

As Barnes stood up, brushing his trousers, he heard two female voices coming towards him. WPC Linda Smythe and Sue Perkins were discussing their conversation with Henrietta as they walked down the hallway from her room.

"Hello, Roddy," said Perkins, "where is the big boss?"

"There's less of him than there used to be," replied Barnes, trying to disguise his embarrassment at being called Roddy, which he liked only slightly more than Roderick, his real name.

"Yes, Colin's embarking on a new health and fitness journey and he certainly looks better for it." Sue Perkins nodded her head to emphasize her approval before continuing, "is he still here or has he left?"

"Inspector Knowles is in Basil's room, I believe, looking for clues about Basil's involvement in the first murder."

"Right," said Perkins, "let's go and find the sleuth and avail him of certain facts about Basil."

"Actually, I have to talk to Fairfax about golf so I will be along later." Barnes indicated he was about to head over to the Hall.

"Suit yourself, Sergeant, see you later," replied Perkins, "which is Basil's room?"

"It's the first on the left," said Barnes and then headed out of the front door.

Perkins and Smythe found Knowles carefully examining the bottom of the cupboard in which Basil's clothes hung.

"Found something, Colin?" asked Perkins.

"Almost certainly, yes, I think he hung up his wet shirt in this cupboard and it dripped onto the wood and discoloured it slightly, but I will let Forensics confirm this. So what did Henrietta say?"

"She thought the password on his phone was his birthday, either 24081995 or 08241995 - some combination of 24th August, 1995. On Friday night, when Toby and she came back from the monastery, she knocked on his door lightly to see if he was awake, but she couldn't rouse him and although she listened carefully she couldn't hear him snoring or tossing and turning in bed. She thought he was out, which wasn't that unusual apparently."

"Where did she think he might have gone?"

"Over to the Hall to see who was around; perhaps he might have played snooker. He was a sociable type."

"And any inkling whether he had murderous intentions towards Edward Pritchard?"

"Well this is the strange thing - Henrietta wasn't completely incredulous when we asked her this question, isn't that right, Linda?"

"Yes, she took the question in her stride, sir, rather than flying off the handle," indicated WPC Smythe.

"Flying off the handle?" queried Knowles.

"Yes, Inspector, when Sue asked the question I thought Henrietta would be really upset with us and accuse us of demeaning Basil's memory, tarnishing his reputation, stuff like that, but she didn't say any of that."

"What did she say?" asked Knowles, who was becoming more exasperated by the second.

"Colin, she smiled and said that Basil was capable of having tremendous crushes on people whom he thought fancied him, for want of a better term. Then when he felt slighted at their apparent rejection of him, he would often swear some kind of revenge."

"Who'd fancy him? Is she trying to tell us that her precious Basil thought Pritchard had a crush on him? That's just plain barmy. Pritchard was a heterosexual. So was Basil gay, then?"

"Not according to Henrietta, but he was very suggestible as regards his feelings," replied Perkins.

"But did Basil talk about Pritchard to her?" enquired Knowles.

"Basil did talk to Henrietta about Pritchard, and this is the strange thing, from what she said I think Basil was more concerned on the effect Pritchard had on her, Henrietta, than the effect Pritchard had on him, Basil that is," explained Perkins.

"And so that could be the motive, right there. Henrietta fell for Edward Pritchard, who wasn't interested in her; she felt upset and Basil, who is sensitive to rejection by the sound of it, was determined to obtain revenge for the slight on her feelings perpetrated by Pritchard."

Knowles stroked his chin and frowned as though he was going over the plausibility of his explanation in his own mind.

"That's an interesting theory, Colin, but wouldn't you have thought that Basil's feelings of revenge would have reduced over time, especially if he wasn't sure when, if ever, he would be able to take that revenge on Pritchard?"

"You would, but perhaps he knew he was definitely coming back up here, maybe for a game of golf with Sir Michael and so he waited for his chance?" Knowles was aware he didn't sound a hundred per cent convincing, but he continued, "Do you think Henrietta could be manipulative?"

"I do," said WPC Smythe, "I think she might have been keeping Basil's feelings of revenge bubbling away by reminding him of how Pritchard hurt her. She might have wanted to kill Pritchard herself, but realised that it would be so much easier if someone else killed him on her behalf."

"That's awfully cold-blooded," said Perkins, "and Henrietta doesn't strike me as that sort, but ultimately you just never know. I would remind you that they are brother and sister - at least I assume they are?"

"Well," said Knowles, "I suppose we should check their birth certificates – Linda, could you do the necessary?"

"I will do, sir," said WPC Smythe, "I'll go and do that now in fact. I will wait for you outside, Sue, if that's OK?"

"Absolutely, Linda, see you outside."

WPC Smythe went out of the room and met Barnes coming the other way.

"Hello, Sergeant Barnes, how are you?"

"Hi, Linda, I am a bit harassed if truth be told, I am not sure what's going on with this case; I don't think either of us even knows for sure how many murderers there are, which is perhaps something you shouldn't mention to any of the people here at the Hall as it wouldn't give them much confidence in the police."

"I am not surprised you say that, because Sue and I spoke with Henrietta a few minutes ago and what she said about her brother was rather odd. She seemed very distant from him and she didn't act as though she was distraught at his passing. It's as though she wasn't surprised this had happened."

"In what way not surprised, Linda - do you mean you think she killed him?"

"No, I don't think she murdered him, but I felt she was expecting this to happen and not necessarily last night either. It's as if Henrietta thought Basil would meet a sticky end."

"That's an odd thing to think about your brother, especially for a teenage girl to think."

"Well, the boss must think there's something odd, because he's asked me to find their birth certificates, just to check they're who they say they are."

"Well, it's best to check, I suppose," concurred Barnes.

"I'll go and start those enquiries, oh...Sergeant Barnes?"

"Yes?"

"I'm fine... thanks for asking." Linda Smythe smiled as she walked away, knowing that Barnes wouldn't understand what she was referring to.

Barnes knitted his eyebrows and stroked his beard, but then remembered he had something important to tell the Inspector and hurried towards the voices of Knowles and Perkins in Basil's bedroom.

"'Allo Barnesy, been having a good natter with Linda?"

"Discussing the case, yes, with Linda, yes," stammered Barnes.

"That's good, that's good to hear," said Knowles, emphasising the word hear, "you look all eager as though you have something to tell us."

"I do, yes. Basil did bring some golf clubs with him as he did on his previous visit three months ago. It seems like Fairfax knocked on the door and entered the room; he almost kicked over the clubs as the room was dark and so he decided to take them to the Hall and place them with the other sets, so that Wilkinson could drive the clubs to the golf course. He then returned and found that Basil wouldn't need the clubs after all."

"That's another example for the book of euphemisms I am going to publish after I retire," said Perkins, laughing at the thought, "did the butler say that or did you, Roddy?"

"I just repeated what Fairfax told me," replied Barnes very solemnly.

"Where are the clubs now?" asked Knowles.

"They're in the Hall along with the other bags; they were never taken to the course."

"Right, go and grab that bag and bring it here. Bring Fairfax with you too. I'd like to know where the clubs were when he almost knocked them over."

"Right, will do, sir," said Barnes and headed back to the Hall.

"Words do carry easily down that hallway, don't they?" said Perkins.

"They do, and I wonder who was able to listen in to our interviews yesterday simply by standing at the front door?"

"Well, I can't help you there, Colin, but I am sure you kept notes of who was interviewed both before and after Basil."

"Undoubtedly, but I was thinking that Basil might have overheard someone else's version of events; he might have stayed around and heard someone lying to us and decided to partake in some blackmail. For example." Knowles shrugged his shoulders.

130

"Yes, Henrietta said he was a bit of a gossip too and so he might have told her or Toby and simply been overheard. Anyway, Linda will be waiting for me outside, so I will see you again in a couple of days, once I have had a chance to think things through."

"Thanks Sue, and if you think of anything important, you've got my number, haven't you?"

"Indeed I have. Young Linda's really good with people, you know, Colin; she's a great listener and intelligent too. You've got a good team together, congratulations." With that Perkins smiled at Knowles and headed outside.

Knowles was pleased with the feedback about WPC Smythe and thought he should start giving her more onerous tasks than checking whether two people were in fact brother and sister.

Sue Perkins was soon replaced by Fairfax and Barnes, who was carrying Basil's golf clubs.

"Mr. Fairfax... Christopher, can you show me where Basil's clubs were when you came in this morning?"

Fairfax retraced his steps to the doorway and mimed opening the door. He walked forwards two steps and then stopped.

"Inspector Knowles, the clubs were approximately here, in the middle of the floor, I almost knocked them over, I can assure you."

"I'm not surprised if they were there - why would anyone place them there in the first place?" asked Knowles.

"Perhaps the murderer moved them?" suggested Barnes.

"In the dark? That would be almost impossible without waking Basil up," replied Knowles.

"But if Basil was already awake then it wouldn't matter; perhaps the light was on too? We've been assuming that the murderer killed Basil in the dark, but perhaps they were talking or had even arranged to meet?"

"I think Mr. George did see a light on in the coach house in the very early morning," said Fairfax, "he told me as much at breakfast."

"Did he now," said Knowles, "right, let's go and talk to him. Sergeant Barnes, when Forensics arrive to inspect

Basil's cupboard and shoes ask them to check that bag for fingerprints. Perhaps the murderer was careless."

"Why are Forensics inspecting his cupboard and shoes?" asked Barnes.

"I have a hunch," replied Knowles, "regarding young Basil's cleanliness and I would like Forensics to check something for me."

=========

When Knowles and Barnes entered the lower study George Johnson was sitting in an armchair, reading a copy of the *Daily Mail* and bemoaning the state of the world.

"Those awful Socialists are ruining the country; building those eyesores called wind farms that blight the view for those of us who enjoy the English countryside."

Gertrude Johnson nodded her head and said, "Yes, dear, they make such a noise when you get close to them."

"Are you referring to the Socialists or the wind farms?" replied her husband laughingly.

"Well, both I suppose, they both whine in their own way."

Knowles failed to suppress a cough that interrupted the flow of the conversation. He didn't care for either the tone of the discussion or the newspaper being read.

"Mr. Johnson, Fairfax tells me that you might have seen someone heading over to the coach house last night and then seen some lights on in one of the rooms. Is this correct?"

"Oh yes, you're Inspector Knowles, aren't you? That's right. I thought I did see someone walk over towards the coach house when I was looking through the window around 1:15a.m. I couldn't sleep, you see."

"And there were some lights on in the coach house at the time?"

"There were, Inspector, in both the rooms I can see from the bedroom window. I watched someone head across the courtyard and noticed the lights were on in the coach house."

"And did you see all this out of just one window?"

"Indeed - I didn't have the light on in our room as I didn't want to wake Gertrude."

"Thank you, Mr. Johnson - is it fine with you if my Sergeant goes upstairs and checks which two windows you can see?"

"That's perfectly fine, Inspector, just so long as he doesn't disturb anything."

"I will be very careful not to disturb anything," Barnes assured the elderly couple and headed upstairs.

"Did the person you saw have a torch with them?" enquired Knowles.

"I think he was playing it in front of him," replied George, "but I got the impression the person knew where they were going."

"And how did you know it was 1:15a.m., Mr. Johnson - I thought you kept your glasses case in front of the alarm clock as the light was too bright for you?"

"That is true too, but I do keep my wristwatch in the bathroom, so I am certain of the time."

"And the watch is definitely working and set to the correct time?"

"It is, Inspector Knowles."

"I just have to check, it's part of my job, it would be remiss of me not to check. Did you recognise the person walking across the courtyard?"

"I am pretty sure it was young Toby, returning to the coach house after playing snooker with his brother. There's always been a great rivalry between them and neither of them likes to lose at anything, even tiddlywinks."

"Would Toby have needed a torch to get over to the coach house?"

"He's a very cautious boy, sometimes," interjected Gertrude Johnson, "he doesn't take many risks."

"But he's hardly navigating his way across a minefield, is he? It's his own courtyard after all."

"Sometimes the horses or dogs can leave their poo for you to step in and that can be upsetting," replied Gertrude.

"That's right," added George as if to emphasise the point.

"How typical of dogs to do that; cats bury their poo so that you don't need to worry about stepping in it."

"Cats don't know the retrieve game though, Inspector."

"Depends on what you mean by game," replied Knowles, "cats hunt and don't need humans to intervene."

"Cats are always playing their own game by their rules anyway," replied Gertrude, "they are far too independent for my liking."

"We are going to have to disagree there, Mrs. Johnson," replied Knowles, "that's the exact reason I think so highly of them. Anyway, you're sure that it was Toby heading over to the coach house?"

"I think I'd recognise my own grandson, Inspector Knowles."

"I know what you mean, Mr. Johnson, thank you for the information. I will go and see what my Sergeant has found out upstairs."

"If we can be of any further assistance, please let us know," said Gertrude.

Knowles nodded his head and left the room. As he headed towards the staircase, he saw Sergeant Barnes coming the other way. They met at the bottom of the stairs.

"So, Barnesy, what's the scoop?"

"Well, sir, we have a tale of two windows. To see Toby walking across the courtyard, George would have looked out of the window that's facing into the courtyard, but this window gives no view across to the coach house. To see lights in the coach house, George would have looked out of another window, which provides a limited view of the courtyard. Also, from the first window you can't see the door that leads into the courtyard from the house, so a potential murderer could come out of the door and keeping close to the wall remain out of sight from that window."

"Good observation, Sergeant Barnes. So he's either imagining the lights on in the coach house or he changed windows, which he didn't mention."

"I should have said that he could see Basil's window and also Henrietta's."

"And he's in the dark all the time without any lights illuminating him from behind," mused Knowles.

"So the murderer must have struck after Toby went over to the coach house as Basil's light was still on?"

"Assuming George isn't confused and did look out of more than one window."

"Right, a big assumption, which we should clear up soon."

"Agreed, I think you should go and clear it up now - by the way, also ask them whether they were shown the exit door of the secret passage on their last visit here three months ago. I think we forgot to do that."

"We should ask Ellis too."

"Agreed - I will do that when I see him. Miss Newton seems to be trying to attract my attention, so I will go and see her whilst you see the Johnsons."

Barnes nodded and headed to the lower study. Knowles went to see Miss Newton, who looked quite upset.

"Eleanor, are you alright - you look as though you've seen a ghost?"

"I have just had one of those deja vu episodes, Inspector."

"We all get those on occasions, Eleanor."

Miss Newton smiled and looked around. She then looked at Knowles and indicated she would like to talk further outside; Knowles obediently followed her into the courtyard. When they were standing by the box topiaries Miss Newton started to speak.

"Inspector, I was just standing outside the hallway entrance to the kitchen when Mrs. Johnson came up to me and asked me for some more lemonade for the lounge...," Miss Newton took out a tissue and dabbed her eyes, "and I was reminded of something similar happening yesterday..."

"With the tonic?" asked Knowles

Miss Newton nodded.

"You remembered who asked you for the tonic yesterday?"

Again Miss Newton nodded and dabbed her eyes.

"And who was it, Eleanor, who asked for the tonic?"

"It was Basil, he asked for the tonic for the lounge."

"He didn't say who had asked him for it?"

"He didn't mention who it was."

"Thank you, Eleanor, for remembering this important tidbit of information."

"I hope it helps."

"I am sure it will."

At that moment the Forensics team vehicle pulled up in front of the Hall.

"Will you be alright, Eleanor, should I ask Mrs. Swarbrick to look after you?"

"I will be alright, Inspector, I wish I'd remembered sooner that's all."

"It wouldn't have made any difference, Eleanor, please don't blame yourself."

"Right, Inspector, I won't, thank you for saying that."

Miss Newton returned to the Hall quietly composing herself for the inevitable interaction with the family and guests.

Knowles greeted the Forensics team enthusiastically. At that moment, Barnes came out of the Hall and headed over to the assembled officers.

"What news, Barnesy?"

"After some thought, George did think he moved from one window to another and he probably switched the light on before doing that so that he wouldn't trip over the bed clothes."

"Thus illuminating himself for all to see."

"Only for two minutes he said."

"Right, and what about being shown the outside exit of the secret passage three months ago?"

"A definite yes from Gertrude - she said they were both shown the exit along with four or five others including Henrietta, Ellis and Basil."

"Interesting, thanks Sergeant - anyway, it's time to round up everyone again in the lower library and question them as a group this time about Basil's unfortunate demise. Please ask Fairfax to organise this on our behalf. I will be along in ten minutes once I have shown these lads the items I wish them to investigate. See you in there, Barnesy."

Knowles led the Forensics team into the coach house and up to Basil's room. Outside the door he explained what he wanted them to do. "Examine Basil's shoes and see whether any of them have recently been extremely wet. They all look polished but I believe one pair were recently made very wet in the long grass near the monastery. Also, please examine his shirts and see if any of them have been recently stained with blood that has been washed out. I think he dried the shirt he washed in the cupboard and some of the water has dripped onto the wood below - the wood has been stained and I think you might find traces of blood there. Does anyone have any questions?"

"Do you want us to take the shoes away or examine them here?" asked Peters, the team lead.

"Whichever is easier for you, I don't mind," replied Knowles, "just find out whether any of his shoes have been really wet recently. Give me a call before you leave and let me know what you have found. If there are no further questions, then I will leave you to it - I am going to the lower library in the Hall to talk to the surviving people."

As he walked across to the Hall, Colin Knowles hoped that the Forensics team would turn up something that would establish one theory above all the others that were swimming around in his mind. He didn't like being so confused about a murder enquiry.

=========

Barnes had asked Fairfax to organise everyone in the lower library. When Knowles arrived most people were settling down in their chairs. George and Gertrude Johnson were the last to arrive and they sat on the sofa by the fireplace. Once they had sat down Knowles started to talk.

"Thank you for all being here at such short notice - as I am sure you are aware, Basil Fawcett was murdered this morning at around 1:30a.m. in his room. If there is anything you can remember that would shed some light on this grisly crime then I would really appreciate if you could speak up now; if you don't wish to talk in front of everyone else, please take me aside afterwards and let me know then. Now, where were you all between 1a.m. and 2a.m. this morning? Let me rephrase it - is there anyone who wasn't in bed between those hours?"

"I wasn't, Inspector," said Cedric, "I was playing snooker with Toby, James and Timmy until about 1:25a.m. and then we dispersed for the night."

"We were in bed," confirmed Sir Michael. Bunny Johnson registered no emotion as he said those words.

"We were asleep at that time," confirmed Ellis Hardaker. Gwendoline smiled and yawned slightly.

"As were we," said George, "apart from when I woke up and saw Toby crossing the courtyard to the coach house."

"You saw me?" replied Toby.

"Oh yes, playing the torch in front of you, just so you wouldn't step in anything unpalatable," replied Gertrude.

"What about you, Cedric?" asked Barnes.

"We played another frame of snooker and then headed off to our room at about 1:40a.m. We were the only ones around at that time. I fell asleep as soon as my head hit the pillow." Cedric smiled at the memory. "I slept like a log."

"I read for a while," said Timmy, "and fell asleep with the book in my hand."

"What were you reading?" asked Knowles.

"*1984* by George Orwell."

"And you, James?" enquired Barnes.

"I was still excited because I won the last frame, so I stayed awake until well after 2."

"Did you hear anyone moving around?"

"Strangely enough I thought I did, but only on the landing and not on the stairs."

"Could that person have gone down the spiral staircase between the libraries, do you think, so as not to make any sound on the main stairs?"

"Quite possibly - are you suggesting I heard the murderer? You are, aren't you? Oh my god, that's horrible."

Timmy Beauregard placed a hand on his brother's shoulder to console him.

"Henrietta - where were you last night?" asked Knowles.

"I was talking to my brother until about 1 a.m. and then I said good night to him, for the last time as it turned out." Henrietta just stared straight ahead and spoke the words without any emotion.

"Thank you, Henrietta, for being so brave," said Knowles. Henrietta smiled weakly. Toby squeezed her hand.

"Mr. Jenkins, where were you?" Barnes turned to address the gardener who was standing in the doorway.

"I was at home tucked up in bed well before midnight."

"Can anyone verify that for you?"

Jenkins smiled. "Unfortunately not."

Jenkins said the two words with such resignation that a few people grinned.

"I'm sorry to hear that, Jim," quipped Knowles, "Mr. Wilkinson?"

"My wife can verify that I went to bed at 11 and didn't wake up until 7a.m. this morning."

"Right, Miss Newton, where were you at that time?

"I was fast asleep; I was reading too last night, and it was *Country Life* before you ask."

"Thank you, and Mrs. Swarbrick?"

"I have to say the same as Jim, on my own - in bed at 10:30 and woke up at 6a.m." No one grinned at Elspeth's matter-of-fact statement.

"And Mr. Fairfax, what about you?"

"Well, I was reading until midnight and then fell asleep until 6:15 when the alarm went off."

"And what book were you reading?" asked Knowles.

"*The Third Girl* by Agatha Christie," replied Fairfax, "I like mysteries."

"Thank you, Mr. Fairfax, well, I have to say I don't like mysteries, I detest them. It goes without saying that at least one of you is lying, unless the murderer is a sleep-walker of course. I will find out who murdered Basil - mark my words. Thank you for your attention. Oh, there is one last thing - who has golf clubs and was intending to play this morning?"

Gradually people put up their hands. Sir Michael, Lady Bunny, Gwendoline, Ellis, James, Timmy, Cedric and Fairfax all indicated they would have been attending the golf.

"Eight people, thank you, you can put your hands down now."

As people started to leave the library, Knowles was approached by Timmy Beauregard.

"Inspector Knowles, can I have a word with you?"

"Certainly, Timmy, how can I help?"

"You said you were going to find out who murdered Basil; surely you meant Basil and Edward Pritchard?"

"I meant what I said, Timmy, I am going to catch the murderer of Basil Fawcett."

"Would you care to explain, Inspector?"

"Not at the moment, but all will be revealed in the fullness of time."

"I see, well, I look forward to seeing the revelation." With that Timmy Beauregard was gone. He was replaced by Ellis and Gwendoline.

"Hello, Ellis, were you looking forward to playing golf?" asked Knowles.

"I always enjoy playing golf, Inspector, and I might still do so this afternoon if that's not against the rules? We aren't under house arrest, are we?"

"Just so long as you promise to come back afterwards. Gwendoline, how are you?"

"I might go with him just to keep him under surveillance," she replied, "I feel so invigorated this morning after a tremendous night's sleep - it must be the country air."

"It must be – well, enjoy your game and I will see you later..." Knowles' phone started to vibrate, "oh, I should take this, it's the Forensics team."

Knowles waved at Barnes who was talking to Miss Newton and indicated he should come over and join him in the sports room.

"Hello, yes, I've finished. I will be over there in a minute; have you found something significant? Right." Knowles terminated the conversation.

"OK, Barnesy, let's go back to the coach house."

The two officers walked quickly across the courtyard, through the ivy-festooned doorway and up to Basil's room.

"So, what have you found here?" asked Knowles as soon as he came through the door.

Peters indicated a pair of brown walking shoes.

"Basil brought seven pairs of footwear for a long weekend, which would be excessive for a supermodel;

however, these are the ones that have been polished recently before they were thoroughly dried out. We found a few specks of dirt under the polish and some dampness too. We'll take a few samples of soil from the refectory and see if they match. There's also some pollen from grass in the laces and on the soles, so again we'll obtain grass samples from the monastery. But these are the ones he was wearing, so we'll take them back to the lab for further tests."

"If those are the ones he was wearing when he killed Edward Pritchard," said Barnes, "why didn't he try and hide them in his suitcase or something?"

"Because he thought polishing the shoes would be enough to cover up his crime. I also believe Basil assumed that the thief wouldn't do anything about Basil taking the sword, but the thief must have seen him either take the sword or use the sword on Edward Pritchard. Basil's number was up at that point, because the thief knew that Basil had seen the thief place the sword in the passage. Basil would have talked eventually. Anyway, Dr. Peters, what have you found out in the cupboard?"

"Why are we investigating the cupboard too?" asked Barnes.

"When Basil stabbed Pritchard with the sword some blood must have splashed on to his shirt, Barnesy, and Basil wanted to remove the blood in case anyone saw it," replied Knowles.

Dr. Peters continued,: "Young Basil did quite a thorough job of washing his shirt but he should have perhaps let it dry in the shower and then he could have removed the drips from the bath with a tissue; I presume he was trying to be secretive by drying the shirt in the cupboard, but those drips did leave a slight stain on the unvarnished wood. It looks like there might be some colouration of the wood, so we will take a sample and see whether there's any blood, and if there is, what blood group it is. We'll also take the shirt and see whether there's any trace of blood on that."

"Thanks, Doc," replied Knowles, "Basil wasn't expecting to have Forensics go over his handiwork so closely. I suppose he thought just washing the shirt would be enough and then he could put it in the washing machine when he returned home."

"I expect he was, but whomever killed him acted quickly, as though this had to be sorted out this weekend - that must concern you, Colin, could anyone else have seen what Basil saw?"

"I am concerned that someone else did see something; after all, the murderer only has to believe that someone might have seen him or her move the sword for that someone to be in severe danger. The murderer is not going to take any chances."

Barnes chimed in, "Is it not also possible that when the thief went to reclaim the sword, but found it missing, that he/she might have been seen? Either near the exit from the secret passage or on their way to or from the monastery?"

"It is, Barnesy, entirely possible, anyway we should leave Forensics be and discuss this over a lunch time pint at the Hart."

"Sounds like a plan, sir."

"Good, we'll need our notes and a large piece of paper so we can draw a diagram. I don't want there to be another murder tonight. Our murderer loves the night time." Before he left Knowles asked Forensics to take a couple of items from the Hall back to the lab. Peters shook his head and almost laughed out loud - this was the most unusual request for information that anyone had ever made. What was Colin Knowles thinking?

Chapter 5

Knowles ordered two pints of Pedigree and took them over to where Barnes was sitting. A sheet of A4 paper was lying on the table with a rough sketch of Manton Rempville Hall and the monastery drawn on it. They were trying to work out who had the opportunity to see Basil Fawcett take the sword from the passage.

As Knowles read out names, Barnes marked their whereabouts between 11:25 and 11:50 on Friday night on the map with a cross and an initial. Individuals' locations were based solely on the statements provided by that person.

"So what do we have, Barnesy?'

"More uncertainty than certainty, I suppose. Gertrude and George were in their bedroom together - asleep admittedly. Fairfax was asleep on his own as were Miss Newton, Jenkins, and Mrs. Swarbrick, Wilkinson was at home with his wife asleep, but he had been out earlier that evening. Lady Bunny and Sir Michael were alone during the earlier part of the time frame, as were Gwendoline and Ellis. Henrietta and Toby were walking together near the monastery, so could have seen Basil. Timmy and James along with Cedric were coming back from the pub around 11:30. They would have been together but perhaps Timmy was looking out of the window with his binoculars towards the monastery or saw someone near the house. He seems interested in what's going on and the precise time of everything,"

"Yes, he's sharp and nosey in equal measure."

"Henrietta and Toby said they thought they might have seen someone in the monastery."

"They did but nothing definite. It's Timmy that worries me the most; Basil's murderer was out and about at the time Timmy might have been looking out of the window for owls."

"Timmy's not the murderer then?" queried Barnes.

"No he's not; he wasn't here last time they all met. He couldn't have thieved the sword."

"Who did Miss Newton see, do you think?"

Knowles downed the rest of his pint before answering. "Eleanor Newton saw Edward Pritchard, who was hanging around the Hall waiting to speak to Lady Johnson I would guess. Pritchard was taking a huge risk, of course, because he was supposed to be meeting the thief in the monastery grounds over an hour later."

"You don't think Eleanor might have stayed out for longer than she told us?"

"Why would she do that?"

"An inquisitive personality, perhaps? She heard the cars come back at roughly the right times, but would she have heard them from her room?"

"She might have, but I don't think she's the murderer of Basil - when she was showing us the exit of the secret passage, I think we were being watched by the murderer and not by Timmy, even though we found the planted chewing gum wrapper."

"In that case, isn't she in danger, sir?"

"Possibly, but only if she stayed out later on Friday night than she told us and so was seen by the murderer of Basil."

"But Miss Newton almost certainly saw the murderer sneaking into the lounge with the sword on Friday afternoon."

"The murderer obviously doesn't know that, Barnesy, because she's not been attacked."

"Might that be a way of capturing the murderer, sir?"

"Let it be known that Miss Newton saw the murderer, wait for her to be attacked, and then jump in between them in the nick of time to save her? That's taking an unnecessary risk with an innocent woman's life. There has to be another way; there must be a clue we've missed. I think it's time we found out more regarding Timmy, James, Cedric, Lady Bunny, Ellis and Sir Michael between 11:30 and midnight."

"Why those six?"

"Because they should have an alibi from another family

144

member or friend for either part or all of that time period and it would be good to get both sides agreeing where they were together and when. Ellis will be more difficult because Gwendoline was in the shower."

"Wait a minute, Sir Michael got back to the Hall at what time? 11:30? I wonder if he parked his car near Ellis' car?"

"You're driving at what exactly, Sergeant?"

"Ha ha - I thought that Ellis Hardaker and Sir Michael would have seen each other, because if Sir Michael did get back at that time then wasn't Ellis sending an email from his car at that time?"

Knowles checked the notes from Gwendoline's interview. "She heard bells between 11:20 and 11:30 and then they stopped. But the bells in the village stopped at 10:30. So, which bells did she hear?"

"Was her watch wrong?"

"We should assume not, but could she have been mistaken, could she have mistaken another noise for church bells?"

"I doubt there's a noise that would be an adequate substitute."

"So, let's find where those bells came from and more importantly when they stopped - which churches are to the east of here?"

"St Timothy's in Goat Parva and All Saints in Flixton spring to mind. What about St Andrew's in Scoresby - would the noise travel that far?"

"Let's assume so, Sergeant. Tell you what, I should take a trip back to the station to see Forensics anyway, so I will have a Sunday afternoon drive via Goat Parva and Flixton. The first stop will be to see our old friend Reverend Strong in Goat Parva."

"Perhaps you should take him some vegetables for the church fund?"

"This will be police business, not a social call."

"And you want me to interview James, Timmy etc. to see whether they can recall where they were on Friday night between 11:30 and midnight?"

"Absolutely. If you can get the three boys to agree on

their whereabouts that would narrow down the suspects."

"Right, that's what I will do - could I have a lift back to the Hall with you?"

"Of course, Barnesy, you may have to be firm with Sir Michael and Lady Bunny as they will resent the intrusion I am sure. Interview Ellis first as I believe he may be playing golf later."

"Sounds like a plan, Inspector."

========

After being dropped off at the Hall Barnes found Fairfax in the lounge.

"Mr. Fairfax, would you know where Ellis and Gwendoline are?"

"They will be playing the first nine holes at Burton Magna at 3p.m. They will be getting ready - would you like me to ask them to spare you a few minutes, Sergeant Barnes?"

"I would like that very much," replied Barnes, thinking how much easier life would be for him if he had someone like Fairfax to make his introductions.

"I will ask them to come and see you in the lounge," said Fairfax, bowing his head slightly.

Barnes went out into the hallway and found himself standing where Miss Newton had been two days previously when she had been arranging the flowers and had thought that the murderer had gone in to the lounge without seeing her. On an impulse, Barnes crouched down like Miss Newton said she had been when the murderer came by and waited to see if he would be spotted. Presently he heard three people come down the stairs and go into the play room. Barnes followed them into the lounge.

Ellis Hardaker turned around and was surprised to see Barnes there.

"Sergeant Barnes, where did you come from?"

"I was in the hallway just checking something."

"Right, well, Fairfax says you wish to ask us some more questions. Can this be fairly brief as we have a tee-off time of 3p.m.?"

"Of course, I will be brief - I need to know some exact times for your whereabouts on Friday night between 11:30 and midnight."

"Right, well we came back at 11:10 and around 11:20 I realised I had to send an email from my i-Pad, which was in the car and so I went back to the car and wrote that email, which was sent at 11:33 - here is the i-Pad so you can check."

Barnes looked in the 'Sent Items' folder and saw that an email was sent at that time with an attachment.

"Fine, and then you returned to the room?"

"Yes, that's correct - it was 11:35 and Gwendoline was just coming out of the shower."

"How long was it until you saw each other?"

"It was 11:42, Sergeant," replied Gwendoline, "I looked at my watch when I put it back on after drying myself."

"But between 11:20 and 11:42 you were out of each other's sight."

Ellis nodded and said "Strictly speaking yes, but for the last seven minutes I was in the room."

"I sensed he was there, Sergeant," added Gwendoline, hugging Ellis' arm, "he was there. He couldn't have possibly gone to the monastery and back in that time. He was still wearing his shoes from dinner and they weren't wet or covered in grass."

"I never thought he had gone to the monastery in that time, we aren't looking for the murderer of Edward Pritchard, but for the murderer of Basil Fawcett. Thank you for your time and I hope you enjoy the game of golf."

Ellis Hardaker looked slightly surprised at what Barnes had said. The couple left the room hand in hand. Fairfax remained behind.

"Sergeant Barnes, is there anything else I can help you with?"

"There is - could you find me Timmy, James and Cedric - I will also need to speak to Lady Bunny and Sir Michael together."

"Of course, they haven't gone out so I should be able to organise that. Will you be staying in here, or will you be hiding behind the table in the hallway again?"

"I will be staying in here, thank you for asking."

Fairfax smiled before exiting the room. Barnes wrote something down in his notebook.

He looked around and noticed that the potted plants had been removed from the room. Barnes also checked to see if any of the windows would open and only one of the ones he tried seemed to open.

"Trying to break out?" asked a voice.

Cedric smiled as Barnes turned around, slightly embarrassed.

"Hello Cedric, are Timmy and James with you?"

"They soon will be, so you want to know about Friday night?"

"Only between 11:30p.m. and midnight. Were you together during that time or within each other's sight?"

"We were, I believe; yes, we came back at around 11:30 in the taxi and then went up to my room and played a few video games together. At least James and I did, I think Timmy was looking through the window for part of the time. Here they are, hey, what did we do on Friday after the pub?"

James and Timmy looked at each other.

"Well we came back here and played that new video game of yours - Minecraft," said James, "except that Timmy just had to look out of the window with his binoculars, because he thought he heard an owl hooting."

"Did you see an owl, Timmy?" asked Barnes.

"I thought I saw someone in the distance near the woods, but they disappeared quickly and so I think it was just a trick of the light," replied Timmy, "I didn't think it was worth mentioning earlier."

"Well you have mentioned it now, which is good," replied Barnes.

"So that's all you wanted to check, Sergeant, that one of us hadn't gone and killed Pritchard after coming back from the pub?" Cedric folded his arms in a defiant gesture.

"It's not Pritchard's murder I am investigating, it's Basil's that's concerning me," confirmed Barnes, adopting his politest tone.

"Interesting," said James, 'well, I hope you catch who did it quite soon."

With that the three boys left the room. They were soon replaced by a decidedly unhappy Sir Michael Johnson and his wife.

"So have you found the murderer yet, Sergeant Barnes?" asked Sir Michael.

"We have found one of them, we believe, but we still aren't sure about the other one. There are two murderers, we believe; Pritchard and Basil Fawcett were murdered by different people."

Sir Michael looked half-impressed. "I haven't seen anyone arrested; are you keeping this quiet?"

"We are trying to, just to reduce the amount of publicity the whole case receives." Barnes was impressed with his answer.

"So what would you like to know, Sergeant?" asked Lady Bunny.

"Your activities between 11:30p.m. and midnight on Friday. How much of an alibi can you provide each other? I have to ask everyone these questions."

"Well, Sergeant, I was in bed by 11:15 and I was reading when Michael returned at about 11:35p.m. I think we switched off the lights around midnight. So we can provide each other with an alibi for most of the time you requested."

"Thank you, Mrs. Johnson; Sir Michael, did you see Ellis Hardaker in his car when you returned to the Hall?"

"I didn't see anyone definite, but then I wasn't expecting to. Your eyes play tricks on you - I could have seen someone over by the monastery, near where the secret passage comes out, but when I looked again there was nobody to be seen. I perhaps should have mentioned it earlier, but I thought I was mistaken and I couldn't have identified whomever it was anyway."

Barnes then remembered another question he wanted to ask.

"Who was the person who visited you at your agent's house on Friday night, Sir Michael?"

"That would have been Wilkinson, who was delivering a

package that he had picked up for me from the Post Office in Scoresby earlier in the day."

Barnes smiled and thanked the Johnsons for their time.

=========

When Sergeant Barnes was talking to the people at Manton Rempville Hall, Inspector Knowles had driven over to Goat Parva to see Reverend Strong. The vicar was well-known to the Inspector as he had played a pivotal role in a previous murder investigation.

Knowles walked into the church and saw Reverend Strong tidying up the church interior after the morning service.

"Inspector Knowles, how wonderful to see you; how can I help you on this occasion - seeking a guiding hand from the Lord?" Reverend Strong had always believed that Knowles was seeking something more than evidence to convict criminals.

"Reverend, it's not a guiding hand from the Lord I am interested in, but the guiding hands of your bell-ringers, who might have been practicing on Friday night. Were they in fact playing that evening?"

"The campanologists don't ring here on Fridays; however I believe they do go to All Saints at Flixton and ring there instead."

"Excellent, thank you Reverend Strong, and who is the leader of this merry band?"

"You should contact Mrs. Edwards in Goat Magna; she lives at The Laurels on the Manchester Road. There are eight ringers in their group."

"I will, Reverend Strong; how are you coping without Carol Herald bringing you vegetables from her garden?"

"Carol, God rest her soul, has been missed in many ways, but the Lord has provided. Brenda Jargoy stepped into the breach and we now have enough food for all our fund-raising events."

"I am glad to hear that you're coping without Carol's contributions, Reverend. Anyway, I'd love to chat some more, but I should drive over to Goat Magna and see Mrs.

Edwards. She might be able to help us in a murder enquiry."

"Oh yes, Inspector, I'd heard that Bingo had been finding bodies again; this one was in Manton Rempville monastery I believe?"

"He's only found one and I'd like to keep it that way, so I should go. It was good to see you again, Reverend Strong."

Reverend Strong smiled and shook Knowles by the hand. Knowles left the church at a quick pace and jumped into his vehicle. Churches made him feel very uncomfortable and he was scared of finding out too much of his spiritual side, or rather he was scared someone else would. There couldn't be a God, could there? At least not an omnipotent God, otherwise He would know that humans were intending to commit murder and by not stopping the act, He was actually condoning the death of one of his own creations.

Knowles drove to Goat Magna and soon found The Laurels, a Georgian house set well back from the road in its own grounds. He opened the gate and heard the sound of classical music emanating from the garden shed. He strode up the path, ignoring the soaring voices on his left-hand side, and knocked on the front door.

The door was opened by a young man aged around thirty. He was wearing a green cardigan and jeans, plus slippers that looked like they'd been bought by an elderly aunt for his birthday.

"Can I help you? Are you with the ringers?"

Knowles smiled and took out his identification, which he showed to the young man. "I am Detective Inspector Knowles from Scoresby CID; could I speak to Mrs. Edwards, please?"

"She's been banished to the shed by my dad, so she's playing The Bells by Rachmaninoff quite loudly."

"I see - well I have to speak to her about Friday night at All Saints in Flixton."

"Oh, did someone complain? I thought we'd got away with it."

"No, you didn't get away with it," said Knowles, sensing there was a confession on the way, "so just tell me what happened."

"Well, Jack was the conductor and he called a full peal rather than a quarter peal, so we didn't finish until 11:25 or just after."

"Jack is a very silly boy then, isn't he? Make sure he doesn't do it again or we will send the Noise Abatement Society around to muffle your bells. I am sure you wouldn't want that."

"We definitely wouldn't, Inspector Knowles; it won't happen again."

"Right, well, thank you for that information – sorry, what was your name again?"

"The name is Leighton, Inspector, Leighton Edwards."

"Thank you for the information, Leighton Edwards."

With that Knowles turned around and walked back to his Land Rover. Gwendoline had heard the bells at 11:25, which placed Ellis outside Manton Rempville Hall at about the right time to be seen by Basil. On the other hand, Ellis and Gwendoline must have come back to the Hall a few minutes before 11:25, so who came back in a car at 11:25? Sir Michael? One of the sets of boys? A nice list of car arrivals would be extremely helpful.

Knowles soon arrived at Scoresby station and headed to the Forensics department. Dr. Peters was carefully examining some shirt fibres under a microscope and another technician was looking at Basil's polished shoes.

Knowles rubbed his hands together and said in a loud voice, "Ladies and gentlemen, what information do you have for me?"

Dr. Peters stood up and beckoned Knowles over to the workbench.

"Inspector, firstly the easy one. The only prints on the golf bag are those of Basil Fawcett."

"Really, so Fairfax wore gloves even when moving golf bags – wow, that's impressive in a way. Anyway, please continue."

"I have found some evidence of blood on the shirt and on the shaving of wood that I took from the cupboard. The blood on the wood was barely traceable, but the blood from the shirt will be enough to give us a match, though whether it's from Edward Pritchard or Basil Fawcett remains to be seen. Basil washed the shirt well but not well enough. Let's see what Jane has found on those shoes."

Knowles and Peters walked over to an adjacent table where Basil's shoes had been dissected with a sharp knife. The laces had been removed.

"Jane, what have you found with the shoes?"

"Well, I collected some grass and soil samples from the monastery before returning and the first indications are that the pollen and vegetative matter found on these shoes, both shoes by the way, matches the grass from the monastery. The treads on the shoes contain some soil which again matches the soil at the monastery. Someone cleaned the bottoms of the shoes with a toothbrush and did a good job, but they probably used too much pressure as they pushed the soil into some slight cracks in the sole and that's where I found it."

"Good job, Jane," said Knowles, smiling broadly, "is there some evidence that Basil polished the shoes before they'd dried thoroughly?"

"Yes, there is - they were almost dry when they were polished and brushed, but it does look like he may have dried them with a hairdryer as there was some unevenness in the drying. You can tell because in some areas the polish didn't adhere too well, but if anyone was inspecting the shoes without too much care they wouldn't spot that."

"Excellent, so it seems certain that Basil headed over to the monastery after returning to the Hall from the pub. The real question is: who saw him on his travels that night?"

"Inspector, we haven't been too successful in the other matter you asked us to look into," said Dr. Peters.

Knowles looked over at the two plants from the lounge at Manton Rempville Hall, which had been removed from their pots.

"What did you find in the soil?" he asked.

"The plants had been well watered and are extremely healthy. We will put the soil back into the pots, so you can take them back to the Hall."

"There was no trace of any tonic in the plant pots? None at all?"

"None at all, Inspector, no tonic."

Knowles smiled to himself and thanked the technicians for their efforts. He waited for the plants to be re-potted and carried them individually back to his Land Rover. Barnes' flashy Morgan would not have been suitable for this task, he thought.

Before returning to Manton Rempville Hall Knowles went back to his desk, wrote down a few items that desperately needed checking, and phoned Barnes to ask him to meet him outside the Hall in half-an-hour. He had a horrible feeling that the killer of Basil Fawcett had another victim in mind and he and Sergeant Barnes would have to move quickly to prevent another death.

========

Knowles drove back to Manton Rempville Hall and parked in front of the topiary box hedge. Knowles looked at the artistry and wondered whose idea it had been to start the ironic gardening. When he had solved this murder enquiry, he was going to find out what motivated someone to impose man-made shapes on nature.

As pre-arranged, Barnes was waiting in the courtyard. The sun was beginning to set as the two men walked into the Hall carrying the plants that had been examined by the Forensics team.

"OK, Sergeant Barnes, we need some more facts. What time did Henrietta and Toby come back to the Hall on Friday night? And did the taxi drop them off at the bottom of the drive or bring them to the Hall? The same questions apply to Cedric, Timmy, and James. Do you know where they are?"

"I think they're in the lounge."

"Right, let's go and find them quickly," replied Knowles, striding into the play room and then the lounge. Barnes had trouble keeping up. The policemen placed the plants on the table just inside the door.

Henrietta and James were laughing at the joint charade Toby and Cedric were acting out in front of them.

154

"It's six words and the second word sounds like turnip?" said Henrietta.

"I thought it was radish," retorted James.

Toby and Cedric acted for a few more seconds before they all became aware of the presence of the police. Four faces towards Knowles and Barnes.

"Hello," said Knowles, "sorry to interrupt, but I was wondering whether your taxis dropped you off at the end of the drive on Friday night or brought you all the way up to the house?"

"Well, ours dropped us off by the front gate," said Cedric.

"Ours too," said Toby, "at around 11:25."

"Whereas our taxi dropped us off at 11:20, a few minutes earlier," said James.

"Thank you," said Knowles, "that's most helpful. Oh, by the way, I think your charade is Pat Garrett and Billy the Kid. The second word sounds like carrot. Am I right?"

Cedric nodded and Toby smiled.

"Where's Timmy?" asked Knowles.

"He was up in our room," replied Cedric.

"Could you go and fetch him, please?"

"I'll text him, Inspector."

"Sergeant Barnes, go and check that Timmy is upstairs."

Barnes trotted off and Knowles turned to the youngsters.

"Could one of you phone him and the others text him?"

James phoned Timmy, but was redirected to his voicemail. The others didn't receive a reply.

"He's probably watching for owls out of the window and has his phone switched to mute," suggested James.

"Does he do that a lot?" asked Knowles.

"He does like bird-watching."

"And did he look out of the window on Friday night when you came back from the pub?"

"I believe he did, but I am not sure he saw anything of any interest."

"Perhaps not, but he may have been seen by someone outside, especially if the light was on behind him."

Barnes returned, slightly out of breath.

"Timmy is not up there and he's not taken his phone with

him as it was lying on his bed. It was vibrating when I got up there. I didn't see any binoculars either."

Knowles took out his wallet, removed a business card, and gave it to Cedric.

"If Timmy returns please phone my cell number on this card at once; I would like to know where Timmy has gone. In the meantime, we will try and find him."

Knowles and Barnes then left the lounge and stopped in the hallway.

"Do you know where Fairfax is by the way, Barnesy?"

"I think he might have gone with the Johnsons to the golf course."

Knowles went into the kitchen and found Mrs. Swarbrick cooking dinner.

"Elspeth, do you know where Eleanor is?"

"I don't, Inspector Knowles," replied the cook, stirring the soup vigourously, "it's her afternoon off, so she's probably gone for a bike ride."

"What kind of soup is that," asked Knowles, "it smells very spicy?"

"It's mulligatawny, Inspector Knowles, and you are quite welcome to have some."

"I'd love some soup, perhaps in a mug, Elspeth. And one for the Sergeant too."

Mrs. Swarbrick ladled steaming liquid into two large coffee mugs and handed them over to Knowles.

"Thank you, Elspeth, this will fill a gap. I think we'll check Eleanor's room and see if she's there."

"Right, well, I'll tell her you're looking for her, if I see her," said Mrs. Swarbrick. As Knowles left, she started to chop the radishes and celery with an expert hand.

"Here you are, Sergeant Barnes, some warming soup for you. Let's go and find out if Eleanor's in her room."

"And if she's not, sir?" said Barnes, sniffing the soup suspiciously.

"We should see if we can look around her room and find out what time it says on her bedside alarm clock."

The two men sipped their soup as they walked over to the coach house. Miss Newton's room was on the ground floor and faced away from the Hall towards the village of Manton Rempville. Knowles knocked on the door and there was no reply. He turned the handle and found that the door was unlocked.

"Well, Barnesy, this seems slightly suspicious to me, but let's just see if she's in here or not."

"Well, sir," replied Barnes, "we are investigating a murder, after all."

Knowles opened the door slowly and peered inside. The room was tidy and quite spartan. Miss Newton's clothes were neatly folded on a small chair and a spare T-shirt was draped on the bed. Knowles checked the bedside alarm and found that the time was correct. The two policemen looked around the rest of the room and the bathroom for a couple of minutes.

"Doesn't this room make you feel rather cold?" asked Barnes.

"It's the blue walls and the black curtains, I would imagine," replied Knowles, "there are no warm colours in here at all."

"Should we perform an in-depth search for anything in here, sir?"

"I don't think so at this juncture, we should go and find Timmy Beauregard if at all possible."

"Where do you think he's gone?"

"My hunch would be over to the monastery to find some owls; have you finished with your soup? I'll take these back to the kitchen and I will catch you up."

"Do you think he's in danger?"

"He might well be if the murderer of Basil suspects that Timmy saw him or her on the Friday heading towards the exit of the secret passage only to find Basil had got there first."

"You maintain Basil saw the thief put the sword in the passage and then took the sword before the thief could use it. Basil then murdered Edward Pritchard but was seen by the thief, who was intending to murder Edward Pritchard, but was beaten to it by Basil. Of course, the thief had to silence Basil in case he told someone. The thief may have looked back at the Hall, seen Timmy, and thought he or she had been spotted."

"That's more or less it, Sergeant. I'm not sure how the thief and Edward Pritchard communicated and arranged to meet, but they must have. I'm also not sure how Basil knew that Edward Pritchard was the intended victim. Anyway, I will take these mugs back to Mrs. Swarbrick and I will see you over there."

Knowles closed the door and they left the coach house. Barnes veered around the south side of the Hall and started to walk towards the monastery. He couldn't see anyone around and then phoned Knowles to ask him to bring a torch with him from the Land Rover.

Barnes was walking the same route that he and Knowles had taken with Miss Newton the day before and this was somehow comforting to Barnes as he headed towards the monastery in the last light of day. He stopped and peered across to the woods to the north and saw a figure heading back to the Hall. Barnes immediately phoned Knowles.

"Sir, there's someone heading back towards the Hall through the woods, could you try and intercept them? I can't tell who it is but I don't think they're carrying any binoculars, so I don't think it's Timmy... Right... OK, I will do."

Following Knowles' instructions, Barnes phoned WPC Linda Smythe and asked her to head over to Manton Rempville Hall with two other constables and to keep their sirens off. They should report to Knowles when they arrived. Barnes continued towards the monastery, stumbling on the uneven surface until he remembered he had a small mini-torch on his key-ring, which provided a little light. He could have used his phone for some illumination but that drained the battery quickly and he decided that he might need to make a few more phone calls before the day was through. After five further minutes he came to the area where the secret passage exited. Barnes shone the torch around and saw that the wooden trapdoor covering the exit was exposed to the elements. One corner was slightly askew, indicating perhaps that the door had been hastily lowered from within.

"Oh no," said Barnes to himself, "someone is heading

back to the Hall underground." He phoned Knowles but there was no reply. He looked back towards the Hall and saw one set of car headlights arriving in the courtyard. *That's probably the golfers returning,* he thought.

He tried phoning Knowles, but again no reply. Barnes headed towards the monastery and stood on the refectory wall. He heard a hoot in the woods and scanned the area with his torch more in hope than expectation. The beam picked up an object lying on the ground just two feet in front of him. Timmy's binoculars had been discarded in a hurry. The strap looked as though it had been ripped out of someone's grip. His phone rang: it was Knowles.

"You've caught Jim Jenkins," said Barnes, "yes, well I have just found Timmy's binoculars at the monastery and I have a bad feeling, because the trapdoor over the exit was exposed and I think someone has gone back to the Hall and will not be seen because the golfers have come back. Perfect timing, almost as though it were planned... Right... I will keep looking for Timmy. Oh, two cars are coming down the drive, that must be our lot. Are you coming over to the monastery... once you've spoken to the troops... Good, it's creepy around here. And please bring a torch."

Barnes rang off and looked down at the binoculars. It seemed as though they had been thrown and Barnes tried to guess the direction they'd come from - he followed his hunch and looked through an arch. He played the fading torch around and saw a human hand clutching a stone. Timmy Beauregard had obviously tried to pull himself off the ground and failed as his body was lying prone. There was a nasty bloody wound on his left temple, but he appeared still to be breathing, although in a very shallow manner.

Barnes immediately phoned for an ambulance and told them to come to the car park at the monastery. He phoned Linda Smythe and asked her to check on Eleanor Newton's room and to send one of the other constables down the secret passage with a torch to see if there was anyone still down there. *Not that there would be but you have to cover all eventualities*, he thought.

Barnes bent down and tried to make Timmy's head

comfortable with his jacket. Timmy was semi-conscious and Barnes tried to communicate with him.

"Timmy, it's Sergeant Barnes, the ambulance is on its way, did you see who hit you?"

Timmy shook his head slightly and grimaced with pain. He whispered, "Binoculars" and mimed throwing something away from him. He then indicated he'd been hit with a stone.

Barnes repeated what he thought Timmy was telling him. "Someone ripped the binoculars from round your neck and then hit you with a stone. They threw the binoculars through the archway?"

Timmy nodded weakly.

"Did your attacker have a torch?"

Timmy shook his head and whispered, "Dark".

Barnes heard someone shouting his name in the distance and poked his head through the archway.

"Over here," he shouted at the top of his voice and waved the torch above his head.

Knowles arrived out of breath a minute later. He handed Barnes a spare torch.

"Have you found Timmy?"

"Yes, he's still alive."

"Attacked with the dagger that was missing?"

"No, with a stone, hit on the temple, we should go and check on him."

"Yes, but where's the dagger gone?" said Knowles.

"I'll see if I can find it, perhaps the attacker dropped it?"

"Yes, and there's no shortage of spare stones, is there - take your pick, whichever is fit for purpose."

Knowles bent over Timmy and smiled. "You're going to be OK; the ambulance is on its way." He then noticed Timmy's watch.

"Eh, Barnesy, the watch has been moved forward and then smashed; it says 6:30 and it's only now 6:15."

Knowles caught Timmy's eye, pointed at the watch and showed him the time.

Timmy looked surprised and mimed the watch being hit with a stone.

"That's odd isn't it, sir," remarked Barnes, "the attacker

has used the same trick as Basil used on Edward Pritchard's watch."

"Who did we mention that to, can you remember?"

"Everyone I believe, I think we told them all when they were gathered together."

"Someone is taking the mickey out of us, Sergeant Barnes, and I don't think it's Jenkins the gardener, even though I did think about arresting him for poaching."

"But who could it be, Inspector?"

Knowles was interrupted by the siren from an ambulance as it arrived in the car park. Barnes ran over towards the paramedics waving his torch and indicating that they would need a stretcher for Timmy Beauregard. While Barnes was helping carry the medical equipment Knowles looked around on the ground, playing the torch into the nooks and crannies of the walls. He was looking for something very specific that did not belong in these surroundings.

The stretcher arrived and after a couple of minutes of quick work Timmy Beauregard was on his way to hospital. The constable who had come along the secret passage had found no one hiding; Knowles had suspected as much as this murderer was far too clever. Tape had been placed around the crime scene and the area would be scoured at first light to see what evidence could be obtained.

Knowles phoned WPC Smythe and asked her about Eleanor Newton. Smythe indicated the door was still open and that Eleanor hadn't returned from her bike ride. Smythe also reported she'd just been told by the Records Office that Henrietta and Basil were truly brother and sister with the same father and mother. Knowles then headed back to the Hall followed by Barnes, who was almost freezing as his jacket had gone to the hospital along with Timmy.

Once back in the lounge, Knowles found Toby reading a newspaper.

"Toby, have you been in here all the time since I left? You haven't left this room at all?"

"I have been in here all the time."

"And no one came past you from the secret passage in all that time?"

"No, I would have heard the noise of it opening."

Barnes came back into the room clutching a brandy and wearing a hunting jacket borrowed from the sports room courtesy of Fairfax, who followed two steps behind Barnes.

"Where's James, Toby?" asked Knowles.

"Upstairs I believe with Cedric, have you found Timmy?" replied Toby.

"We have, yes, he has been attacked but he's still alive," replied Knowles. "Mr. Fairfax, one of my constables will drive James and anyone else who wants to go, to the hospital. Sergeant, could you tell James what happened? Thank you."

"Will do, sir," replied Barnes.

"Toby, is Henrietta around? Is she in her room?" asked Knowles.

"She said she was going there, yes. After you left she suddenly felt tired and wanted a lie down."

"I will go and see Henrietta. Mr. Fairfax, who came back with you from the golf course?"

"Sir Michael, Lady Johnson, Mr. Ellis and Miss Gwendoline."

"And you and Wilkinson? All in one vehicle?"

"Yes, that's correct."

"And you have all been together for the last hour or so, no one slipped away for a few minutes at any time?"

"Absolutely not, Inspector."

"Thank you, Christopher. That narrows things down somewhat."

"Is Mr. Jenkins under arrest? He seems to be handcuffed to a chair in the lower study."

"Oh, I forgot about him, leave him be for a moment or two, I want to see Henrietta first."

"Right you are, Inspector."

On his way outside Knowles poked his head into the kitchen and saw Mrs. Swarbrick, who was still cooking dinner.

"Hello, you haven't seen Miss Newton I take it?"

"No, I haven't, she's out a bit late actually."

"Is she now? Well, I'll have another look for her."

With that Knowles closed the kitchen door and crossed over to the coach house.

He reached Henrietta's room and knocked on the door quietly. There was no reply and so he knocked a bit harder. He heard some stirring and the door was opened by Henrietta in her stockinged feet.

"Hello, Inspector, how can I help you?"

"Did I wake you? Sorry, but I thought you'd like to know that we found Timmy. He's been attacked but he's still alive and has been taken to hospital."

Henrietta shook her head and started to sob. "Who's doing this, can't you catch them?"

Knowles looked apologetic. "We are doing our best; we are narrowing down our list of suspects."

"That's probably because the number of people left alive and in good health is reducing on a daily basis. It's like the Agatha Christie story *And Then There Were None*."

"I think that's an exaggeration; anyway, if you wish to visit Timmy in hospital my constable will be driving people over there in a few minutes."

"Thank you, Inspector Knowles; I will head over to the Hall when I have put my shoes on."

Knowles smiled and walked towards Miss Newton's room. When he was about ten yards away, Eleanor came out of her room and started coming towards him.

She had showered and was wearing her serving clothes.

"Eleanor, we were looking for you earlier, did you have a nice bike ride?

"I did, Inspector, I was just going to check I'd locked my bike."

"I am sure it will be fine - I will check it for you, how about that? I think you should go to the kitchen - Mrs. Swarbrick was concerned you were out a bit longer than normal."

"Really, well that's the first time I've heard of her being concerned at my well-being."

"Yes, well people change sometimes. Where did you go on your bike?"

"I rode over towards Goat Parva and Flixton…"

"... And you rode past the monastery?"

"It's difficult not to if you head eastwards, Inspector."

"Indeed, so did you see anyone near the road on your way back, someone carrying a bloody stone with them? A stone that delivered a grievous head wound to Timmy Beauregard?"

"Timmy Beauregard has been attacked at the monastery? Who by? I didn't see anyone."

"There's not many people it can be, Miss Newton."

"Who do you think it is, Inspector Knowles?"

"I don't have any proof of who it is, so it would be unfair of me to say at this stage."

"Right, well in that case, I should go and help Mrs. Swarbrick serve dinner, especially as she has been so concerned about my health."

Knowles watched as Miss Newton walked off in a hurry. He and Barnes should now interview Jim Jenkins - Sir Michael would not appreciate his gardener being handcuffed to an expensive chair for very long.

Two minutes later Knowles went back to the Hall and found Barnes standing on the main staircase looking down at the table in the hallway.

"We should talk about that in a few minutes, Barnesy, but first we should talk to Jim Jenkins in the lower study, see what he has to say."

Knowles walked into the room and sat in front of Jenkins, who was staring out of the window.

Barnes came into the room. "PC Clement is driving James, Cedric and Toby to the hospital to see Timmy; do you have any questions for them?"

Knowles shook his head and said, "No, none of them are suspects, unlike our friend here, who very much is a suspect." Barnes smiled and slipped out of the room.

Jenkins looked at Knowles. "I was walking through the grounds and I didn't hear anything."

"What were you doing in the woods, Jim?"

"Minding my own business."

"You were just going for a walk then, Jim, just a walk in the woods. And that was the only reason you were there?"

164

"I was just going for a walk; I wasn't aware that was a crime?"

"Did you see anyone, Jim?"

"I saw your Sergeant walking out of the Hall before you arrested me. Before that I thought I saw someone on the Goat Parva side of the monastery, but I didn't recognise them."

"What time was that?"

"Around 6p.m., roughly."

"Did you move the exit to the secret passage so that it was slightly askew?"

"No, I wasn't on that side of the monastery. Why would I do that anyway?"

"To confuse us, Jim, which you have certainly achieved."

"Why are you asking me these questions anyway, Inspector?"

"Because Timmy Beauregard has been attacked."

"Is he still alive or has he been killed too?"

"He's still alive, but he's going to be in hospital for a few days undergoing tests I would imagine."

"Who would do that to him? He's an inquisitive lad but harmless. Likes the birds, doesn't he? I have seen him with his binoculars."

"Yes, I think you've found the reason he was attacked. He saw something he shouldn't have. On Friday night just after he came back from the pub."

"Saw something through his binoculars?"

"Presumably, yes."

At that moment Barnes returned to the room.

"They've just left for the hospital, sir, should we take Jenkins here back to the station for further questioning?"

"No, that won't be necessary, Sergeant Barnes, I don't think Mr. Jenkins here is a suspect after all in the murder of Basil and attempted murder of Timmy. We should release him without further ado."

Knowles leant over and unlocked the handcuffs.

Jenkins flexed his arms and looked at Knowles.

"What did I say that convinced you I wasn't a suspect?"

"Well, Jim, you obviously had no idea about the exit of the secret passage being left askew. Our attacker deliberately wanted us to believe they'd gone down the passage back here, while they disappeared in another direction. You wouldn't leave the exit askew and then walk back through the woods because you would be spotted, as indeed you were by the Sergeant here."

"Right, well, honesty is the best policy, I think."

"Yes, Jim, you're right. Anyway, you may go and leave the two of us here as we have to discuss something."

Barnes closed the door behind Jenkins as he left.

Barnes pointed at the door. "If it's not him, then who exactly is left as a suspect?"

"Well, Barnesy, there's only one person it can be."

Knowles named the person and Barnes asked him how he intended to find out.

Two minutes later Barnes went to the lounge and told everyone present that the police were leaving for the day to go and interview Timmy Beauregard, but would be back tomorrow. Meanwhile, Knowles made two phone calls. At 8:30p.m. they left the Hall in Knowles' vehicle.

========

"Who was left at the Hall, Sergeant?" asked Knowles.

"Mrs. Swarbrick was still cooking in the kitchen as there had been a delay for some reason; Henrietta didn't go to the hospital as she still felt tired; Miss Newton was there, as was Fairfax. Sir Michael was in the lounge with George, Gertrude, Gwendoline and Ellis. Jenkins and Wilkinson had gone home and the rest were at the hospital."

"Lady Bunny went to the hospital?" queried Barnes.

"Yes, she did - anyway I hope you're right about this, sir," said Barnes, crouching down behind a wall, "otherwise this could be a long night."

"That's why I asked Linda to fetch some supplies. Hot soup, sandwiches, and some warm clothes. I hope I am correct too, Barnesy, but I do think that she will come and look for that knife, because she seems to assume the worst and will worry that there will be some fingerprints on it or some telltale thread."

166

"How can you be confident that she was going to use a knife?"

"Because I found the knife, actually the dagger we were missing, when we were here previously today when Timmy was attacked. I shone the torch around and saw a glint in the stones. Obviously, she couldn't shine a torch around when she was here as that would have highlighted her presence."

Barnes was open-mouthed in astonishment.

"What's the matter, Sergeant, are you hoping to catch your dinner?"

"You could have told me, you could have, you know."

"True, but you would have probably given the game away by glaring at her or something similar."

"Why not arrest her at the Hall?"

"By bringing her back to the scene of the crime we show that she knew where the attack took place and that she was prepared to commit murder with the knife she was looking for. Why come out here looking for something that she's supposed to know nothing about?"

"I see, well that does make sense; I can't see Linda at all - she's good at blending in to the background."

"Let's hope the others are too."

"How long do you think we will have to wait, sir?"

"Not long, Sergeant, she doesn't know when the search team will be arriving, does she? So, the sooner the better. I think we should keep our voices down just in case and keep your phone covered up if you take it out of your pocket as it will stand out like a beacon in this dark place."

Barnes looked around the walls with the weeds growing on top and shivered as the wind blew some branches in front of the moon.

"Do you think she'll come down the secret passage, sir?"

"I think that could prove difficult as she will have to bypass the people in the lounge, so I expect her to come across the grass and rough ground between here and the Hall."

"They'll have finished their dinner now, so she can make her excuses and leave for the night and so won't be missed. Which way will she come over here?"

"On the north side; coming the south way will take her past the Hall and she might be seen. Keep those binoculars trained on the woods to the north of the Hall."

A minute later Barnes spoke.

"Well, well, speak of the devil; I think we have a suspect heading our way."

Knowles looked through the binoculars and confirmed what Barnes had said. He radioed everyone to be ready in ten minutes.

Barnes watched as the suspect headed through the woods, around the back of the monastery, and entered the grounds via the stile on the public footpath. The suspect walked through the archway and started to search amongst the rocks on the ground using a small torch.

WPC Smythe took some pictures of the suspect on her camera.

Knowles radioed everyone that he was about to confront the suspect and so they should all close in to make sure escape was not an option.

Knowles stood up slowly and walked to the archway entrance.

He took the dagger in its plastic bag out of his coat pocket and held it up.

"I think this might be what you're looking for."

The figure turned around and was immediately illuminated by three police torches. In spite of this, the suspect hurled their torch at Knowles, who moved just in time.

"The game is up, Eleanor, we know it was you, too many things just didn't add up."

Miss Newton shook her head and looked around for a stone to throw.

At that moment an owl swooped down low over Knowles causing him to cover his head with his arms. Miss Newton saw her chance to run past Knowles and head for the secret passage, which she reached with unerring accuracy. She opened the exit door and climbed down into the passage, throwing aside the ladder as she reached the floor.

As Miss Newton raced to the secret passage Knowles

called Manton Rempville Hall and the phone was answered by Fairfax.

"Christopher, it's Inspector Knowles, listen please go to the lounge and ensure that the passage is locked - please do that now and I will wait for you. Thank you... Hello, it was open but is now closed. Really. Yes, the reason is that Miss Newton is heading towards you right now and I don't want her to access the Hall. Why? Well I am attempting to arrest her for murder and attempted murder. Yes, both - she has been busy. On no account let her in. Despite what she may say, she has no weapons and no hostages. Thank you, Christopher. Please can you remain in the lounge until you hear either myself or my Sergeant ask you politely to open the door... Right, see you soon."

Knowles arrived at the passage exit and found that one of the constables had jumped into the passage and replaced the ladder against the wall.

"Do you want me to go first, sir?" asked Barnes.

"Thanks for offering, Barnesy, but I will go first - I hope that my torch lasts the distance; she won't be able to get through the door at the other end - I asked Christopher to lock it; it seems like the door was open, which shows how slick Miss Newton is."

Knowles shone his torch ahead of him and walked quickly down the passage - he kept reminding himself that there were no hiding places for Miss Newton to use.

After six minutes Knowles heard a raised voice demanding that she be let into the Hall. Soon the torch picked up Miss Newton pounding her fist quite weakly against the wall. She was sobbing.

"Let me in; who locked the door - I unlocked it before I went over to the monastery."

"The game is over, Eleanor - there's no way out and no owls to help you escape this time."

Miss Newton nodded her head and slumped down onto her haunches.

Barnes moved up and grabbed her arms whilst Smythe put handcuffs on.

Knowles knocked on the door and shouted, "Christopher,

it's Inspector Knowles, please open the door, we have apprehended Miss Newton."

There was a creaking sound and the entrance into the lounge opened.

"Why did Timmy Beauregard have to come here? Why? He should have stayed at home like last time," screamed Miss Newton as she was escorted to the police van that had now arrived at the Hall.

Knowles told WPC Smythe that they'd interview Miss Newton straightaway at Scoresby CID. Miss Newton would also need a lawyer.

========

As they headed towards Scoresby, Knowles and Barnes talked through their thoughts on Miss Newton.

"I think you and I both had our suspicions about her," began Knowles, trying not to pat himself on the back too much.

"Well it gradually accumulated, didn't it, sir? Crouching down behind the table when the murderer went into the lounge."

"She would have been seen by anyone who was on the watch for other people."

"Telling us that Basil Fawcett asked for the tonic to be replenished around 6p.m. and yet Fairfax actually replenished it less than five hours later."

"There was no tonic in the plants and only Bunny Johnson likes G and T."

"Telling us that one car arrived back at the Hall on Friday at 11:10p.m. and the other at 11:25p.m. 11:10p.m. was accurate, but 11:25p.m. was not."

"And yet she claims to have looked at the same clock when both cars arrived."

"When we were at the exit to the secret passage with her and I said we were being watched she said 'It's probably Timmy Beauregard'. How would she know that he watched through binoculars given that he didn't come up here three months ago?"

"Right, given that she wouldn't have seen him with his binoculars that morning as we interviewed everyone just after breakfast and then she showed us the exit immediately afterwards."

"When he came up here on Friday he went to the pub straightaway after arriving in the late afternoon, so the only time she could have seen him was when he came back from the pub and was in his room looking towards the monastery."

"Which means she must have been where he was looking, i.e. at the monastery."

"Finding that Basil had taken her carefully hidden sword and then looking back to see a figure with binoculars looking towards her."

"Remember that Timmy said in his interview that she shared his love of birds; she obviously had to find out which of the three boys in that bedroom was using the binoculars that night. A love of birds, which would make a visit to the monastery to see the owls at dusk an easy suggestion to make and she would be waiting for him dagger in hand ready to strike."

"Unfortunately, no one has seen her at the scene of her crimes; being near the monastery when someone else commits murder is not a crime."

"Hence the need to get her out at the monastery."

"Which is what happened - thankfully you found that dagger she was intending to use on Timmy."

"Miss Newton made one mistake and paid for it."

========

In Interview Room Number 1 at Scoresby police station, Eleanor Newton sat staring at the wall. Her legal aid lawyer sat beside her.

Knowles and Barnes came into the room, sat down at the table and switched on the recording device, stating the date and time of the interview.

Knowles began the interview.

"Eleanor, I would like to know what you were doing out at the monastery this evening?"

Miss Newton smiled. "I was going for a walk looking for owls in the monastery grounds."

"These are presumably owls that nest on the ground amongst the rocks and stones in the ruined walls?"

"That's right, Inspector, the burrowing owls I believe they are called."

"Try again, Eleanor, there are no burrowing owls in this country - they're found in the Americas."

"That's why I didn't find any then."

"You were looking for the knife that you dropped earlier when you were about to attack Timmy Beauregard, the one that's being examined now by our Forensics team who will find either your fingerprints or fibres from your clothing on that knife. Or perhaps both because we all know you were extremely careless regarding that dagger, which was why you had to find it before we did."

"I don't know what you're referring to," replied Eleanor.

"Why were you intending to kill Edward Pritchard?" asked Barnes.

"I wasn't intending to kill anyone, Sergeant." Miss Newton was beginning to sound testy.

"You were, Eleanor, you had to kill Basil because you knew he must have seen you move that sword, although you didn't see him. That worried you and so Timmy had to be killed too, just in case he saw something on Friday night when you were near the exit of the secret passage."

"This is simply not true."

"Why did you get the time of one of the cars arriving on Friday night incorrect, Eleanor? One car arrived at 11:10p.m. and the other at 11:30p.m. You said the second car arrived at 11:25p.m., which you would have known if you'd been by your clock, but you weren't, were you? You were out by the exit to the secret passage."

"It's not a crime to misremember the time a car arrived, is it, Inspector Knowles? It's only five minutes."

"You are so precise and correct about everything else, Eleanor, and it is suspicious if you get one time correct but not the other."

"Why is that?"

"You can remember one time accurately but not the other; it suggests you didn't see the second time on your clock."

"Suggestions don't make me a murderer or an attempted murderer. I got the time wrong."

"When we all went to see the location of the secret passage and Barnesy saw someone looking at us through binoculars, why did you tell us it was probably Timmy Beauregard'?" asked Knowles.

"Because I'd seen him with his binoculars previously."

"Previously, define previously, when precisely did you see him with his binoculars?"

"On Saturday morning before breakfast."

"You're guessing, Eleanor."

"No."

"Yes, because when we interviewed Timmy Beauregard after the murder of Edward Pritchard, he specifically said he'd only had one chance to use his binoculars as he and his brother had gone straight to the pub the previous evening. He'd had a quick look out of the window after returning from the pub and he'd not seen any owls but might have seen a figure over by the monastery. That was you, wasn't it? On Saturday morning you had to find out who you'd seen looking at you, so some bird conversations had to be started pretty quickly. I presume you knew it wasn't Cedric and you would have seen James three months previously, so my guess would be you started with Timmy and found out it was him. Time for the dagger. In Cluedo terms, Miss Newton with the dagger in the monastery. Only you mislaid the dagger and I found it."

Miss Newton shook her head.

"You told us that you saw the murderer when you were bending down under the hallway table, yet if you had been where you said you were you would still have been seen by any alert person and I am sure that the murderer would have been on the alert given that he was carrying a large sword."

Miss Newton again shook her head, but tears were beginning to well up in her eyes.

"And another thing," continued Barnes, "you told us that Basil had asked for some more tonic for the lounge on

Friday, but only five hours later Mr. Fairfax had to replenish the tonic for Lady Bunny Johnson. There was no tonic in any of the pot plants."

"Perhaps the person who prompted Basil to ask for the tonic was a heavy drinker?"

"A very heavy drinker who would have been inebriated very quickly, but no one had a hangover on Saturday morning, not even those who'd been to the pub."

"Another coincidence, Inspector, not really evidence though."

"Will you admit that you murdered Basil Fawcett in his bedroom in the early hours of this Sunday morning and that you attempted to murder Timmy Beauregard in the monastery this evening around 6p.m.?"

"No, I will not," said Miss Newton.

Barnes' phone started to vibrate and he went out of the room to answer.

"What will you say, Eleanor, when Timmy says that you attacked him?"

"Why would Timmy say that when I didn't attack him?"

"Do you have an alibi for the time period 5p.m. - 6:15p.m. earlier today?"

"I was riding my bike to and from Flixton and Goat Parva as I told you earlier."

"And did anyone see you, anyone at all who can identify you?"

"I was quite on my own for the whole time."

Barnes came back into the room.

"Well, Sergeant," asked Knowles, "do you have any news for us?"

"I do, sir, I'd like to ask Eleanor a couple of questions if I may."

"You may as well, Sergeant, because I don't have any further questions right now."

"Thanks, sir. Eleanor, when you went on your bike ride this afternoon, what route did you take? Did you go along the major road all the way?"

"I did, Sergeant."

"You didn't take any shortcuts along woodland trails?"

"I didn't, no."

"Strange, then, that you would have some dirt in the tread of your wheels that matches a sample that we had already taken from the monastery grounds."

"It must be old dirt."

"It's fresh, quite fresh; we took it out of your bike's tyres as soon as you left the Hall this evening. It matches a sample taken from Basil Fawcett's shoes as a matter of fact."

Miss Newton breathed in quite noticeably.

"The next question is how far did you ride this afternoon?"

"It's about twelve miles roughly I think, give or take a mile."

"So why does your odometer say two miles?"

"You took that off my bike, you bastard, you shouldn't steal things from me."

"When I met you this afternoon," said Knowles, "you were going back to your bike, weren't you, but I diverted you to the Hall instead - we took the odometer then and photographed it in situ too just for reference. You thought you were safe when Barnesy made his announcement about leaving for the evening and so you didn't go back to the bike, did you?"

Miss Newton folded her arms.

"And the final item, Eleanor, is that Forensics have found a thread of fibre on the dagger that matches your cycling gloves," continued Barnes, "which is presumably why you went back to the monastery to find the dagger."

"All in all, Eleanor," said Knowles, "I believe that there is more than enough evidence here to convict you of the attempted murder of Timmy Beauregard. Why don't you tell us what happened from the beginning?"

========

"When Edward Pritchard arrived it was like a breath of fresh air blew through the fusty surroundings of Manton Rempville Hall. He was very charming and I really wanted to go out with him and be his girl, but he decided to try and be a social climber and so I wasn't good enough for him. I really resented this of course and so I pestered him and tried to persuade him I was the one, but he rejected me and then made up some stupid story about me and Cedric being lovers. This rumour endangered my job of course and so I decided that if I couldn't have him no one could. When everyone was here three months ago I took the sword when the display cabinet had been left open by Mr. Fairfax, I hid it in the secret compartments in the upper study until everyone was away at the golf and then I moved the sword to my room and waited. Edward was fired and dumped by his upper-class women, but I kept in occasional contact with him and let him know that everyone was returning for this weekend. I suggested he should try and make contact with Lady Johnson and Gwendoline. I also arranged to meet him at the monastery on the Friday night. During the day, I moved the sword to the secret passage, but I must have been seen by Basil. Imagine my horror when I get to the exit, I see Basil disappearing into the distance brandishing the sword. I look around and see someone looking at me through binoculars from the Hall. Turns out it's Timmy Beauregard. They both have to go, of course. Basil was easy. He'd just switched off the light and I went in with the knife - I did thank him for murdering Edward for me, but he had to go. I went into his room in my bare feet."

"Did you plant the *Practical Hunting Blade* magazine in Basil's suitcase?' asked Knowles.

"I didn't plant anything in his suitcase; it was too dark to see very much - in fact I almost knocked over his golf clubs, but just managed to hold them upright. I was glad I was wearing gloves otherwise there would have been some nice prints for your Forensics team to find."

"Thank you, Eleanor, please continue."

"Timmy went to the monastery looking for owls at dusk, based on my suggestion. I took the dagger on Friday afternoon from the same cabinet I took the sword from using the keys from the kitchen. However, I was careless. In the ruins I tripped up over a protruding stone and the dagger fell into the wall somewhere. I couldn't use a torch as I would

176

have drawn attention to myself. There were plenty of stones around and I hit Timmy with one of the smaller ones, but I saw someone heading in my direction with his torch giving him away, so I left Timmy behind, reasoning that he hadn't seen my face when I attacked him. I moved the exit door to the secret passage slightly to confuse whomever it was and give me more time to escape. Obviously the someone turned out to be Sergeant Barnes."

"Well your ruse certainly worked," said Barnes, smiling.

"When do you think Basil saw you moving the sword?" asked Knowles.

"I walked down the passage in the late afternoon on Friday and hid the sword in the archway, but I had to hollow out the brick more than I thought I would have to so the handle would fit - I'd already worked out where I was going to hide the sword by the way, and when I was doing this the exit door was lifted off and Basil climbed into the passage. He shone his torch along the passage and I was pretty sure he illuminated my face briefly. I ran back to the Hall, but I was worried he had known it was me moving the sword."

"He probably found the sword at that time," said Knowles.

"He might well have done, but he got to the sword before me later in the evening and did my dirty work for me. I was still worried he would implicate me in some way, so he had to be dealt with."

"Which he was, of course."

"Yes, he was."

"How did Basil know you were intending to meet Edward Pritchard - I can't figure that one out?"

"Well, Inspector, I phoned Edward on the Friday afternoon around 6p.m. to check that he was still able to meet later and I think that Basil must have heard me down the corridor because he and Henrietta arrived at that time. That's all I can think. I used those throwaway phones you can buy to phone Edward occasionally and he would always answer the first time as it was a number he didn't recognise."

"That explains his phone records. Anyway, thank you, Eleanor, I think we have heard everything we need to hear," said Knowles, "so I will formally bring this interview to an end. I will ask Sergeant Barnes to accompany you upstairs where you will be formally charged with the murder of Basil Fawcett and the attempted murder of Timmy Beauregard."

Miss Newton nodded her head and then began to cry as she was escorted upstairs by a uniformed constable and Barnes.

========

After a good night's sleep Knowles and Barnes drove over to Manton Rempville Hall to ensure the Forensics team had access to Eleanor Newton's room and her belongings.

As usual they parked outside the topiary and Barnes headed over to the coach house to see Forensics. Knowles looked at the strangely shaped hedges and shook his head. Gwendoline came out of the Hall and walked towards Knowles.

"You look confused, Inspector Knowles," she said.

"Yes, I am - I don't understand this ironic gardening at all." replied Knowles.

"It was Edward's idea you know, to shape the box hedges into the shape of boxes. I think he was a very talented artist myself."

"I suppose he must have been to have done this, which shows he had some good points."

"He had many good points, Inspector; they were somewhat overshadowed by his ambition to be someone in the community rather than a sub-gardener here at the Hall. He allowed his ambition to dominate his talents and that led to his downfall."

"I think that's true of society as a whole," said Knowles, "and I think we will all pay for it in the end. When ambition overcomes talent too often then only bad things can happen."

And with that Knowles looked out towards the monastery and wondered how the ghosts of the monks were feeling about so much violence being perpetrated in their house of peace.

He was shaken out of his reverie by his phone ringing.

"'Allo, Linda, what's happened? Not another one... on a

train? Really... at Flixton? Tell me that dog isn't involved -
oh good, well we'll be over in a few minutes."

"It looks like there's been another suspicious death, this
time on an excursion train, Gwendoline, so we shall have to
leave you in peace. Au revoir and good luck for the future."

"Thank you, Inspector Knowles; I hope you solve that
crime too."

"Thank you, I am sure we will, I will just go and get
Barnesy and we'll be off."

Gwendoline smiled and turned around to head back into
the Hall. Knowles walked over to the coach house to find
Sergeant Barnes. Knowles knew that Barnes liked steam
trains and so Knowles was sure this latest mystery would be
greatly to his Sergeant's liking.

CPSIA information can be obtained
at www.ICGtesting.com
Printed in the USA
BVHW030724160221
600231BV00001B/90